AL CAPONE
DOES MY
SHIRTS

Al Capone Does My Shirts

Gennifer Choldenko

G. P. Putnam's Sons • New York

ACKNOWLEDGMENTS

All errors are mine and mine alone, but I would like to thank the many people who helped me with this book.

Lori Brosnan and the GGNRA Rangers on Alcatraz Island, Eugene Grant and Myra and George Brown, Nicole Kasprzak, Charles Kasprzak, the Autism Research Institute, Elizabeth Harding, Jacob Brown and Barb Kerley, the Mill Valley and San Francisco crit groups and the books by Jolene Babyak and Roy F. Chandler.

And most especially thanks to the truly amazing Kathy Dawson. If I were Charlotte, I would weave "Some editor" in the corner of her office.

Copyright © 2004 by Gennifer Choldenko.
All rights reserved. This book, or parts thereof, may not be reproduced in any form without permission in writing from the publisher, G. P. Putnam's Sons, a division of Penguin Young Readers Group, 345 Hudson Street, New York, NY 10014. G. P. Putnam's Sons, Reg. U.S. Pat. & Tm. Off. The scanning, uploading and distribution of this book via the Internet or via any other means without the permission of the publisher is illegal and punishable by law. Please purchase only authorized electronic editions, and do not participate in or encourage electronic piracy of copyrighted materials. Your support of the author's rights is appreciated.
Published simultaneously in Canada. Printed in the United States of America.
Designed by Gina DiMassi. Text set in Caslon.
Library of Congress Cataloging-in-Publication Data
Choldenko, Gennifer, 1957–
Al Capone does my shirts / Gennifer Choldenko.   p. cm.
Summary: A twelve-year-old boy named Moose moves to Alcatraz Island in 1935 when guards' families were housed there, and has to contend with his extraordinary new environment in addition to life with his autistic sister.
[1. United States Penitentiary, Alcatraz Island, California—Fiction.
2. Alcatraz Island (Calif.)—History—Fiction. 3. Autism—Fiction.
4. Family problems—Fiction. 5. Brothers and sisters—Fiction.]
I. Title.   PZ7.C446265 Al 2004   [Fic]—dc21   2002031766
ISBN 0-399-23861-1
9 10 8

To my sister,
GINA JOHNSON,
and to all of us who loved her—
however imperfectly.

Table of Contents

Part One

1. Devil's Island 3
2. Errand Boy 7
3. Trick Monkey 13
4. American Laugh-nosed Beet 22
5. Murderers Darn My Socks 29
6. Sucker 35
7. Big for Seventh Grade 42
8. Prison Guy Plays Ball 48
9. Nice Little Church Boy 53
10. Not Ready 60
11. The Best in the Country 64
12. What About the Electric Chair? 71
13. One-woman Commando Unit 80
14. Al Capone's Baseball 87
15. Looking for Scarface 90
16. Capone Washed Your Shirts 98
17. Baseball on Tuesday 103
18. Not on My Team 106
19. Daddy's Little Miss 109
20. Warning 117

Part Two

21. It Never Rains on Monday 125

22. **Al Capone's mama**   130

23. **She's not cute**   135

24. **Like a regular sister**   140

25. **My gap**   143

26. **Convict baseball**   147

27. **Idiot**   149

28. **Tall for her age**   154

29. **Convict choir boy**   159

30. **Eye**   165

31. **My dad**   171

32. **The button box**   174

Part three

33. **The sun and the moon**   179

34. **Happy birthday**   186

35. **The truth**   192

36. **Waiting**   195

37. **Carrie Kelly**   199

38. **What happened?**   205

39. **The warden**   212

40. **Al Capone does my shirts**   215

Author's Note   217

Notes   227

INDUSTRY BUILDING
Capone does
laundry here

THE
CELL HOUSE

REC YARD
Capone plays
ball here

GUARD TOWER
(with crapper)

BACK STAIRS
TO REC YARD
Route
cons take
home from
work

PIPER'S HOUSE

THE PARADE GROUNDS
Annie and I play
catch here

THE MORGUE
(hidden by cell house)

OFFICERS' CLUB
We bowl here

APT. 2E
I live here

APT. 2G
The Mattamans'

THE DOCK

APT. 3H
Annie's

ALCATRAZ ISLAND (1935)

PART ONE

1. DEVIL'S ISLAND

▪▪▪▪▪▪▪▪▪▪▪▪▪▪▪▪▪▪▪▪▪▪▪▪▪▪▪▪▪▪▪▪▪▪▪▪▪

Friday, January 4, 1935

Today I moved to a twelve-acre rock covered with cement, topped with bird turd and surrounded by water. Alcatraz sits smack in the middle of the bay—so close to the city of San Francisco, I can hear them call the score on a baseball game on Marina Green. Okay, not that close. But still.

I'm not the only kid who lives here. There's my sister, Natalie, except she doesn't count. And there are twenty-three other kids who live on the island because their dads work as guards or cooks or doctors or electricians for the prison like my dad does. Plus there are a ton of murderers, rapists, hit men, con men, stickup men, embezzlers, connivers, burglars, kidnappers and maybe even an innocent man or two, though I doubt it.

The convicts we have are the kind other prisons don't want. I never knew prisons could be picky, but I guess they can. You get to Alcatraz by being the worst of the worst. Unless you're me. I came here because my mother said I had to.

I want to be here like I want poison oak on my private parts. But apparently nobody cares, because now I'm Moose Flanagan, Alcatraz Island Boy—all so my sister can go to the Esther P. Marinoff School, where kids have macaroni salad in their hair and wear their clothes inside out and there isn't a chalkboard or a book in sight. Not that I've ever been to the Esther P. Marinoff. But all of Natalie's schools are like this.

I peek out the front window of our new apartment and look up to see a little glass room lit bright in the dark night. This is the dock guard tower, a popcorn stand on stilts where somebody's dad sits with enough firepower to blow us all to smithereens. The only guns on the island are up high in the towers or the catwalks, because one flick of the wrist and a gun carried by a guard is a gun carried by a criminal. The keys to all the boats are kept up there for the same reason. They even have a crapper in each tower so the guards don't have to come down to take a leak.

Besides the guard tower, there's water all around, black and shiny like tar. A full moon cuts a white path across the bay while the wind blows, making something creak and a buoy clang in the distance.

My dad is out there too. He has guard duty in another tower somewhere on the island. My dad's an electrician, for Pete's sake. What's he doing playing prison guard?

My mom is in her room unpacking and Natalie's sitting on the kitchen floor, running her hands through her button box. She knows more about those buttons than it seems possible to know. If I hide one behind my back, she can take one look at her box and name the exact button I have.

"Nat, you okay?" I sit down on the floor next to her.

"Moose and Natalie go on a train. Moose and Natalie eat meat loaf sandwich. Moose and Natalie look out the window."

"Yeah, we did all that. And now we're here with some swell fellows like Al Capone and Machine Gun Kelly."

"Natalie Flanagan's whole family."

"Well, I wouldn't exactly say they're family. More like next-door neighbors, I guess."

"Moose and Natalie go to school," she says.

"Yep, but not the same school, remember? You're going to this *nice* place called the Esther P. Marinoff." I try to sound sincere.

"*Nice* place," she repeats, stacking one button on top of another.

I've never been good at fooling Natalie. She knows me too well. When I was five, I was kind of a runt. Smallest kid of all my cousins, shortest kid in my kindergarten class and on my block too. Back then people called me by my real name, Matthew. Natalie was the first person to call me "Moose." I swear I started growing to fit the name that very day. Now I'm five foot eleven and a half inches—as tall as my mom and a good two inches taller than my dad. My father tells people I've grown so much, he's going to put my supper into pickle jars and sell it under the name Incredible Growth Formula.

I think about going in my room now, but it smells like the inside of an old lunch bag in there. My bed's a squeaky old army cot. When I sit down, it sounds like dozens of mice are dying an ugly death. There's no phonograph in this apartment. No washing machine. No phone. There's a radio cabinet, but someone yanked the workings out. Who gutted the radio, anyway? They don't let the criminals in *here* . . . do they?

So, I'm a little jumpy. But anybody would be. Even the silence here is strange. It's quiet like something you can't hear is happening.

I think about telling my best friend, Pete, about this place. "It's the Devil's Island . . . *doo, doo, doo.*" Pete would say in a deep spooky voice like they do on the radio. "Devil's Island . . . *doo, doo, doo*," I whisper just like Pete. But without him it doesn't seem funny. Not funny at all.

Okay, that's it. I'm sleeping with my clothes on. Who wants to face a convicted felon in your pajamas?

2. ERRAND BOY

....

Saturday, January 5, 1935

When I wake up, I feel kinda foolish, having slept with my shoes on and my baseball bat under the covers with me. My mom's banging around in the tiny hall outside my room. I stick the bat under my bed.

"Where's Dad?" I ask.

"Right here," my dad answers from the living room. He's sitting on the floor with Natalie, holding a pile of buttons in each hand.

"Dad! Could you show me the cell house, and then maybe could we play ball?" I sound like I'm six and a half now, but I can't help it. He's been gone forever and I hardly got to see him at all yesterday. It's lonely in my family when he's not around.

His smile seems to lose its pink. He puts Natalie's buttons down in two careful piles, gets up and brushes his uniform off.

I follow him into the kitchen. "You're not working *today*, are you?"

"I'm having a devil of a time setting up extra circuits in the laundry."

"Yeah, but you worked last night."

My mom squeezes by to run her hands under the tap. "Your father has two jobs here, Moose. Electrician and guard."

"Two," Natalie calls from the living room. "Two jobs. Two."

Doesn't anyone in this family believe in private conversations?

"I could help you . . . ," I offer.

He shakes his head. "You're not allowed in there. Convict areas are off limits to you kids," he says.

"I'm not a kid. I'm taller than you are."

"Go ahead, rub it in." He laughs. "But at least I don't have those big feet either. They're an affliction, those feet." He grabs my head and knocks on it.

"I haven't seen you for three whole months," I say.

"Two months, twenty-two days, twenty-two days," Natalie calls out.

"That's right, sweet pea. You tell him!" my father calls back.

"I'll bet you took Natalie out this morning, didn't you?" The question comes shooting out before I can stop it.

"Oh, for goodness' sake, Moose." My mother looks up from where she's jammed in the corner, scrubbing the icebox. "You weren't even up."

"That isn't fair," I say, though I know better.

"Don't talk to me about fair, young man. Don't get me started on that one." My mother glares at me.

"I'm sorry, Moose," my father says. He reaches for his officer's hat and settles it on his head. "There's nothing I'd like better than to spend the day with you. You know that." His eyes look at me, then quick away.

"Wait, wait, wait . . . you're leaving *now*?" I ask.

He groans. "Afraid so. But there will be plenty of time to spend together. I promise, buddy, okay?" He smiles, kisses my mom and Nat good-bye and heads for the door.

I watch him walk by the front window, his head bobbing like his foot hurts.

My mom glances at her watch. "My goodness, is it that time already? Moose, I need you to watch Natalie while I take the boat to the city. I have to get groceries and arrange an ice delivery," my mother says.

"Ice?" I ask.

"We can't afford an electric refrigerator. We got to keep this one." She taps the old icebox.

"They have a grocery downstairs, though, right?"

"Doesn't have much. Try to do some unpacking while I'm gone. Eleven, twelve and thirteen are all your stuff." My mother points to the crates, each numbered by Natalie. She takes off her apron and puts on her coat, her gloves and her hat.

"You're leaving now too?" I ask.

"I'll be back as soon as I can. Take good care of her, okay?" My mom grabs my arm and squeezes it.

I know she's thinking about what happened on the train yesterday. I had gone to take a leak, and when I came back, Nat was kicking and screaming. She pulled a curtain off the rod and sent her button box flying down the aisle. My mom had her arms around Nat, trying to keep her from hurting anyone. The conductor and the motorman were yelling. People were staring. One lady was taking pictures.

My mom finally got her calmed down by sitting on her right in the middle of the train aisle. I don't know which was more embarrassing, Natalie's behavior or my mother's.

Sometimes Nat's tantrums go on and on for days and nothing makes them stop. It's impossible to know what will set her off. She looks pretty peaceful now, though.

"Sure, Mom." I follow her to the door. "I didn't really mean what I said about it not being fair that Natalie got to go out with Dad this morning. I didn't. You know I didn't. . . . Mom?"

She sighs. "All right, Moose. Just keep your eye on Natalie, okay?"

I watch her leave. A haze rises from the bay like a wall of gray closing me off from everything.

In the kitchen, I find a casserole dish I don't recognize. *Thought you might enjoy some manicotti. Looking forward to meeting you.— Bea Trixle,* the card says.

The manicotti tastes like big fat spaghetti with pizza inside. I'm going for fourths or maybe it's fifths when I hear the knock.

"Don't answer it," I yell to Natalie as I wade through the boxes to the front door. The last thing I want is to meet new kids when Natalie's around. New people don't understand about her. They just don't.

"Open up!" a girl cries. It's a little kid—a short person, anyway. That's all I can make out through the window.

"No!" I call back. But too late. Natalie is already there. She has both hands on the knob and all her weight rocked back on her heels, trying to get the door open.

"Don't open it!" I shove my weight against the door.

"Come on, you know you're gonna!" the girl outside says.

Oh, great. I have little Eleanor Roosevelt on one side of the door and Natalie-the-screamer on the other. What they say about females being the weaker sex is the biggest lie in the world.

It doesn't matter that I weigh more than both of them put together. I know when I'm beat. I let Natalie open the door.

The girl outside has black curly hair that's flat on one side, as if she slept on it. She's missing half of her teeth. The ones she has seem either too large or too small for her mouth.

"How old are you?" she demands.

"Twelve."

"No, you're not!" she says, walking right in without bothering to ask.

"Why would I lie about how old I am?"

She bites her lip, like she's thinking about this. "You got a big neck."

"You're supposed to get a long nose if you lie, not a big neck."

"No." She shakes her head as if she's absolutely certain I'm wrong.

"And you're what . . . seven?"

"Seven and one quarter. Hello, Natalie." The girl smiles her big tooth, little tooth, gap tooth smile. "Your dad told me all about her," she whispers.

We both look at Natalie. Her hair is like mine—brown and blonde all mixed up like birdseed. Different eyes, though. Mine are brown. Hers are green like the marbles nobody likes to trade away. But the way she holds her mouth too open and her shoulders uneven and one hand clamps down the other . . . people know. They always know.

"How old is she?" the girl whispers.

"Ten," I answer. Natalie's age is always ten. Every year my mom has a party for her and she turns ten again. My mom started counting Nat's age this screwy way a long time ago. It was just easier to have her younger than me. Then my mother could be happy for each new thing I did, without it being another thing Natalie couldn't do.

"What's your name, anyway?" I ask.

"Theresa Mattaman. I'm supposed to show you around. You haven't seen *anything* yet, have you?"

"We just got here last night."

"Natalie, come on! We're going now! Run get her coat!" Theresa orders.

I'm big as a linebacker, and a seven-year-old girl treats me like her errand boy. Does she smell weakness on me?

Still, I want to get a look at this weird little island. And what do I care what a bunch of criminals think, anyway? I scribble a note to my mom to tell her we've gone out and prop the paper between the ketchup and the cod-liver oil.

"Come on, Nat. It's not everybody who gets to live down the street from thieves and murderers, you know."

3. TRICK MONKEY

The first thing I see when I walk out the door is the guard tower. I wonder what you're supposed to do here. Should I wave?

Theresa pays no attention. The tower might as well be a tree for all she cares.

She leads us to the stairwell. Natalie's walking behind us with her head down, dragging her left foot on the edge of every step as if she's marking it with her toe. I want to take her hand to make sure she keeps up, but nobody touches Natalie.

"First, we're going to the morgue," Theresa announces with a little skip.

Sure. I've been to hundreds of morgues. Thousands of them, in fact. "Dead criminals . . . don't I get to meet any live ones?" I ask.

"We're not really supposed to talk to the alive ones, but looking for dead guys is my job. *Piper said.*"

"Dead-criminal checker. Sounds like an important position to me. And who is Piper, anyway?" I ask.

"Piper? She's Warden Williams's daughter. She's bossy."

Just what I need, another bossy girl.

"Oh, no, I almost forgot." Theresa claps her hands, then digs in her pocket for a card folded in fours. "I made this for you. Annie did the words. I made the map *all by myself*!"

"And who is Annie?"

"Annie's Annie. She's twelve. She helps me with stuff."

"Are there any boys on this island?"

"Jimmy and"—she counts on her fingers—"eleven little boys who are five, four, three, one and zero."

"Zero?"

"Not one year yet. Do you want to know their names?"

I shake my head, but too late. Theresa is already rattling off the name of every little boy here.

"Thanks, Theresa." I cram the card in my pocket.

"Hey," she hollers in my face, "you didn't read it!" She holds out her hand and wiggles her fingers. "Give."

I hand the card back and Theresa reads it to me.

Alphonse Capone AKA: Scarface,
Big Al, Snorkey.
Born in: New York, January 17, 1899.
Family: Wife named Mae. Son named Sonny.

Theresa reads really well for a little kid, except it doesn't seem like she can walk and read at the same time. Now we're at a complete standstill on the steep road that leads to the top of the island. "Couldn't we do this *after* the morgue?" I ask.

She ignores me. Clearly there's no stopping her until she's read every last word.

Business: Bootlegging gangster mob boss.
Favorite colors: Canary yellow and pea green.
Favorite jewelry: $50,000 diamond pinkie ring.
Favorite weapon: Thompson machine gun.

<u>Favorite crime:</u> Dinner party of death! Invites lieutenants in his organization known to have double-crossed him to a party. After dessert, Al's men lock the doors and Capone beats the traitors to death with a baseball bat.

A baseball bat?

<u>Favorite word for murder:</u> "Rub-out"—often in front of many witnesses who then develop "gangster amnesia."
<u>Sent to jail for:</u> Tax evasion.
<u>Other stuff:</u> Rigged elections. Opened first soup kitchen in Chicago. Likes silk underwear.

What is this guy . . . nuts?

<u>Current home:</u> Alcatraz Island.

"And that's not all we have here either," Theresa says when I look up. "There's Machine Gun Kelly, who happens to be a world-famous kidnapper, and Roy Gardner, who has escaped 110 times, but not from Alcatraz—not yet, anyway. Oh, we have everyone who is bad. Except Bonnie and Clyde on account of their being dead," she says.

A truck horn beeps and we move off the road. A guard in a dark gray uniform like my dad's is behind the wheel. He brings the truck to a squeaky halt and cranks down the window.

I glance back at Natalie, who has been so quiet, I almost forgot she was there. She's looking at the ground as if she lost something. Her arms are down at her sides, not up high like a chipmunk's the way they usually are.

"They Cam Flanagan's kids?" the guard asks Theresa.

Theresa nods. "Yes, sir, Mr. Trixle," she says.

"Where you headed?"

"Piper's house, sir."

Mr. Trixle nods. "Make a beeline there, Theresa. You know the rules."

"Yes, sir."

The guard's eyes scan me and Nat. If he gets there's anything different about her, he doesn't let on. The brakes squeal as the truck inches down the steep road.

Now, the cell house is looming over us like the world's biggest school for bad boys—the kind of place where guys go in and never come out. I wish Pete were here. Pete would love this.

Theresa chatters on about why she thinks Capone will really like her when she meets him, which clearly she hasn't done, yet. The road cuts back away from the water tower. We follow it a short way up to a little cottage. It looks cute, almost like a playhouse. The sign above the glass door reads MORGUE.

Inside, there's a bucket on the floor and a metal box. What do they do in morgues, anyway? Are they like bread boxes for dead bodies? Or do they label stuff in special compartments . . . baskets for fingers? Drawers for toes?

"So, this is it," Theresa says. "Only they keep it locked." She pulls on the door handle to show me.

"Yeah, I see. Maybe we should, uh, move on. Didn't you tell the guard guy we were going to Piper's house?" I don't like getting in trouble. I was born responsible. It's a curse.

Then another girl's crusty voice comes out from the shadows behind the morgue. "What's the matter with your sister?"

My chest gets tight. The blood rushes to my head.

The girl comes around the side of the building, flipping a flat yellow hat on her finger like a pizza. My face turns red just seeing her. She's a looker. If Pete were here, he'd whistle.

"She retarded?" the girl asks.

"None of your business," I tell her.

The girl has freckles and full lips like a movie star. She winds her long dark hair around her finger and looks at me through half-shut eyelids. Something about the way she does this makes me glance down to make sure my fly is buttoned. When I look up again, she's staring at Natalie.

"Stop looking at her like that!" I say.

"That's Piper. Remember? I told you about her!" Theresa says.

"So, not retarded. Stupid, then?" Piper asks.

"Look, could we drop this already?"

"I'm just asking a simple question," Piper says.

"Not in front of Natalie," I whisper.

She shrugs and walks behind the morgue. Theresa and I follow. Nat stays put.

"How would you like it if I asked, are *you* stupid?"

"I would just say no." Piper flips her hair behind her shoulder.

"No, she's not stupid," I say.

"Prove it."

"Uhhh." I clench my fists. I'd really like to give this Piper girl a pounding.

"See, I knew she was retarded," Piper tells Theresa.

"Will you kindly just shut up!" I roar louder than I intend.

They both stare at me.

"Follow me." I walk back around to the front of the morgue.

"When's your birthday, Piper?" I ask.

"November sixteenth."

"1922?"

"Yep."

"Natalie, what day of the week was Piper born?"

"Thursday," Nat says without looking up.

"That right?" I ask Piper.

Piper doesn't answer, but her eyes open wider. She chews at her bottom lip. "What else can she do?" she asks.

"She's not a trick monkey."

"She'd never make it as a trick monkey. She only has one trick," Piper says.

"487 times 6,421 is 3,127,027," Nat says.

Everything is quiet except the sound of gulls squawking overhead and wind rattling a window somewhere. Natalie inspects the ground. It's almost as if she hasn't said anything.

"How much is 28 times 478?" Piper asks.

"13,384," Nat answers.

"Okay, so she's good in math. But *something* is wrong with her," Piper says.

"WHAT IS YOUR PROBLEM?" I shout.

Theresa motions for us to step away from Natalie.

"Natalie lives in her own world. That's what Mr. Flanagan said," Theresa whispers. She takes a jar of jam from her pocket, unscrews the lid and offers us some. We shake our heads no and she dips an already purple-stained finger inside. "Sometimes it's a good world and sometimes it's a bad world. And sometimes she can get out and sometimes she can't."

Piper snorts. "Sounds to me like she's just plain crazy," she says in a low voice. "My dad isn't going to like this. He's not going to like it one bit. He always says the cons in the bug cage are the scariest ones, because you never know what they'll do."

I get a sinking feeling in my gut. There were 237 electricians who applied for the job my dad got. If it were me, I'd have kept my mouth shut about having a daughter like Natalie. What if the warden doesn't know about her?

"She's leaving in a week or two. Going to boarding school. She won't be around here at all. You probably won't ever see her again," I say quickly.

Piper raises her eyebrows. "I'm *expected* to tell him stuff like this. He depends on me to find out things." She places her flat hat on her head and begins hiking up the steep road toward the cell house.

"Wait! Can we come? Can we?" Theresa calls after her.

"Good idea," Piper calls over her shoulder. "Then my father can meet Natalie *himself.*"

My stomach sinks. How am I supposed to know if Nat's a big secret or not? Nobody tells me anything.

"Natalie," Piper calls out sweetly, "would you like to meet the warden?"

Nat says nothing.

"Hey! Come on!" Theresa motions with her whole arm. "Piper said it was okay!"

"I'm going back, Theresa. My mom will be home soon."

"Oh, no!" Theresa cries. "You haven't seen *anything* yet!"

I shake my head. "Maybe tomorrow."

Theresa stamps her foot.

I can't help smiling at this. "I'm sorry, Theresa."

"Ohhhhkay. We'll finish tomorrow," Theresa says in a small voice.

"We gotta go back," I tell Natalie. She doesn't look up, doesn't seem to hear.

"This way." I motion for her to follow. She ignores me.

Oh, swell. Now Nat's acting up.

"Come on, Nat." I try walking down the hill, hoping she'll follow.

She doesn't.

I walk back up to the morgue and sit down on the cement slab by a little dab of something red. Blood? Or is it Theresa's jam?

I figure I'll just wait Nat out when I hear footsteps on the road. "Natalie, come on," I plead.

"Moose!" My mom's voice. She's half running in her high heels. "What in heaven's name are you doing out here?" My mom stops, her chest heaving from the climb. She looks at me, then Nat, then me again. "What happened?" she asks.

"It's okay, Mom. Nat's fine."

"I didn't know where you were." Her voice goes up and down like hiccups. She grips her arms like if she doesn't they won't stay on. "It scared me when you were gone like that."

"I left a note."

She nods. I don't know if this is because she saw my note or because she didn't.

I touch her elbow and try to sound like Dad. "Everything is going to be all right."

My mother nods short and fast. She pushes at the corner of first one eye, then the other, and keeps nodding. Nodding and nodding and nodding.

4. AMERICAN LAUGH-NOSED BEET

∎∎

Sunday, January 6, 1935

The next morning when I get up, I'm happy to find my father at the table, reading the paper.

I can feel how pleased he is to see me. This isn't something you can fake. "Hey," he says.

My mother is checking my sister's suitcase. I can't believe she's going today. I thought it was a week away at least.

Nat has the kitchen chair pulled into the living room, wedged between three crates. "Hey, Natalie, the sun get up okay this morning?" I ask like I do every morning.

She never answers, which used to really bug me. I hate being the brother of a stone. One day last year, I got so mad, I just walked right by her, didn't say anything. Not one word.

That day, after I left for school, my mom said Natalie sat outside my room and cried for two straight hours. Natalie isn't a crier, she's a screamer. You never see her cry for plain old hurt. I'd say my mom made it all up, but she didn't know I'd snubbed Natalie. My mom had no idea why Natalie had cried.

Now I ask Natalie about the sun every morning and it only bothers me a little when she doesn't answer.

"So, what would you like for breakfast on this very special day?" my mother asks her.

"Lemon cake," Natalie says. She says this every day too.

And every day, my mom says, "Silly sweet pea, you can't have lemon cake for breakfast."

"Why not? On a special day like today, lemon cake sounds like a fine idea. What d'ya think, Moose?" my mom asks.

"Sure," I say. My voice comes out high like a girl's. I never know whether I'm going to sound like Mickey Mouse or the giant on top of the beanstalk.

Natalie turns all the way around and looks me straight in the eye in that weird way she has of suddenly being present after weeks of being somewhere else.

"Don't look at me, this wasn't my idea. If it were up to me, we'd be in Santa Monica right this very minute," I say under my breath.

My father reads Natalie headlines from the newspaper, adding numbers to every one. "Work resumes on the Golden Gate Bridge. 103 men are put back to work, two quit, seven scratch their heads, five have their feet up, two eat sausages for supper, three do not . . ."

"Breakfast!" my mother calls.

Natalie holds her face two inches from the plate. She eats so fast, it gives me a stomachache. When my dad's not around, I don't eat with her.

"Natalie Flanagan's whole family," Nat says when I sit down.

I wonder if she knows what's happening. We've built the Esther P. Marinoff up like it's quite the place, like maybe the king and queen of England are sending their kids there too. But somehow in all this talking, we ignored the major thing.

You don't come home from the Esther P. Marinoff. Every morning when the sun comes up, that's where Natalie will be.

My father wipes his wide mouth with his napkin. "What fun you're going to have, Natalie, with kids your own age."

What age is that, I wonder. But I know what he means. Maybe she'll meet other kids like her. Maybe they'll recognize each other and communicate in their own peculiar way.

When my mom has Nat ready to go, my father picks up her suitcase, hands Natalie her button box and opens the door.

"Moose," my mom says as if she's just now noticed I'm here. "I don't think you need to come along."

"Fine with me. I don't want to go, anyway." I don't look at her, or my dad or Natalie.

"Helen!" My father's voice has a sting to it.

"I just didn't think he'd want to, Cam," my mother says.

"Of course Moose is coming." He hands Nat's suitcase to me and pats me on the back. "We can't do this without him."

This reminds me of the time when I was six and my mom shipped me off to live at Gram's. She packed every pair of underwear I owned and she made it all seem like a big treat. When we got there, my gram had an awful scowl on her face. She gave me a big hug and glared at my mother like I'd never seen her do. When my mom left, I heard Gram and Ed talking. "Some cockamamie psychiatrist decides the problem is Natalie doesn't get enough attention, and Helen ships him off! Our Matthew! I'm happy as a pig in mud to have him here, but it's a darn fool thing. What child doesn't have a brother or sister? Half the world has seven or eight. Having a brother didn't make Natalie the way she is. One look at the two of them together and that big-shot psychiatrist would have known that. He's the one ought to have his head examined. It's going to make Nat sicker just having Moose gone."

Early the next morning my father woke me. "Get your pillow, Moose," he said, snapping the buckles on my suitcase. "We're going home."

We're walking down to the dock now. Natalie is going extra slow. I worry we'll miss the boat, but maybe that's her plan.

I like to think all these years have been part of her plan too. And one day Nat will tell me it's all a crazy game she made up to see if we really loved her.

My father jogs ahead. Yesterday the boatman told us, "We don't wait for nobody. Even God himself has to get down here on time." But somehow the big ex-army steamship called the *Frank M. Coxe* is still there.

My mother walks through the snitch box—a metal detector designed to make sure no one is bringing guns on the island.

"This new school is a good opportunity for you, Natalie," my mother tells her as I watch the boat guy unwind a rope, as thick as my arm, from the cleat. "You are such a lucky girl to have this chance."

Natalie says nothing. Her eyes are trained on a gull wiggling a potato chip out from the wood slat bench. I look up at another bird high in the blue sky. And another skimming low over the green blue sea.

My father has a book with him, *McGregor's Illustrated Animal Book*. He's brought it because it has a good index. Nothing pleases Natalie more than having him read the index of a book to her.

"American Leaf-Nosed Bat, page 48," my father reads. "American Quail, page 232, American Spiny Rat, page 188 . . ."

Tons of gulls are flying above our boat. We watch them,

Natalie and I. Natalie is rocking more than usual, but it doesn't look out of place here. The boat rocks anyway.

"I count 229 birds," I say, pointing at the gulls.

"Bad Moose," Natalie says. "Nine birds. Nine."

I smile at her. "I count forty-seven people on the deck."

"Bad Moose, eleven peoples. Eleven." Natalie loves catching my mistakes.

Once when I was seven or eight, she started bringing books to me—big old ones like the dictionary and the encyclopedia. She'd turn to the back and plunk the book on my lap. I couldn't figure out what she wanted. One day, just to get her to go away, I started reading the page she had opened. It was a history book, and the index was full of names of people and places. I got to this one, Machu Picchu, and I said something like, "Mack-who. Pick-you." "Bad Moose," she said. "Ma-chew, Pee-chew." I thought she was nuts until my mom informed me that is how it is pronounced. My mother went straight to the library and checked out a big stack of history books for Natalie. But it didn't take long to realize it wasn't history Natalie was interested in. It's indexes she loves. Any subject will do. We still don't have any idea how she learned the correct pronunciation of Machu Picchu, though.

We're coming into the dock in San Francisco now. Twelve minutes to get to Alcatraz, twenty years to get back, my dad says the cons say.

We sit a minute watching a churchgoing family walk down the gangplank. The toddler goes backward, hanging on the handrail and cautiously moving his squat legs down plank by plank. Everyone smiles at how careful he is. "Going to be an insurance man when he grows up." His dad winks at my mom.

"All right, troops, move 'em out," my father says, but my mom seems stuck in her seat. She's staring at the toddler, who is walking across the dock, holding tight to his mom's hand. My mom blows her nose with her handkerchief. She's blinking fast, trying to keep back her tears.

When Natalie sees this, she curls up in a tight little ball on the wood slat seat and will not move. My mother pulls herself together and tries to sound cheerful again.

"Natalie, honey, I have a little cold. That's all, sweet pea. Now, come on, sweetheart! *This* is a wonderful day!"

Her voice sounds fake and Natalie knows it. She pulls her knees tighter into herself. My father whispers that he hopes he won't have to carry her.

He squats down on one knee and talks to Nat for a long time. The boatman nods to my mother and taps his wrist, to signal time to get off. My mother fusses with her gloves, pulls her hat brim low and walks across the deck to talk to him.

I shift my weight from one leg to the other and back. Finally my father's head pops up. He looks at me. "Moose, can you get her up?" he asks.

"Everyone who is getting off needs to GET OFF!" the boatman booms as people begin boarding for the trip back to Alcatraz.

I look around, searching for an idea. I grab the book and flip to the back. "American Laugh-Nosed Beet, page 3,000," I say.

Natalie is still curled up tight. But her head cocks a fraction of an inch.

"Australian Quill, page 200," I say.

Now she makes a noise deep in her throat and bolts up. "No, Moose! American Leaf-Nosed Bat, page 48. American Quail, page 232!" she says.

I take a step toward the gangplank. "American Spiny Rot, page 18," I say.

"Bad Moose. Bad, bad, bad. American Spiny Rat, page 188." She shakes her head. But she is standing now, following me.

Step by step, page by page, I get her off the boat. Now my dad has the brown suitcase, my mom is smiling and Natalie is next to me. She finds my hand. She grips my fingers together so hard, it hurts.

Natalie has held my hand maybe once before in my whole life. Why does she pick now for this?

This is the right thing to do, I tell myself. But I don't believe it. This is another one of my mother's crazy ideas.

I feel sick to my stomach. I want to pull my hand away, but I don't. I keep walking. Good Moose. Obedient Moose. I always do what I'm supposed to do.

5. **MURDERERS DARN MY SOCKS**

▪▪▪▪▪▪▪▪▪▪▪▪▪▪▪▪▪▪▪▪▪▪▪▪▪▪▪▪▪▪▪▪▪▪▪▪▪▪▪

Same day—Sunday, January 6, 1935

I keep thinking about when my mom's second cousin Mrs. McCraw came to visit. "Put her in an asylum, Helen. It's the humane thing to do," Mrs. McCraw said between bites of cinnamon nut cake. My mom turned ashen. She told Mrs. McCraw she wasn't welcome in our home ever again. Mrs. McCraw took giant gulps of air and tried to apologize, but my mom stood firm, holding the door open. She didn't say a word until Mrs. McCraw limped out, her handbag bumping against her side. After she was gone, my mom found Mrs. McCraw's knitting bag. She sent me running after her to give it back.

"I can't help if your mom can't see the forest for the trees. She's got one good boy, why not focus on him? But no, she goes on these wild-goose chases. It's too bad the child is sick. But cut your losses. No use throwing good after bad."

I nodded then. I didn't mean to. Really I didn't. My neck nodded without my telling it to. But once I'd nodded, I couldn't un-nod. I was too stiff to move. When Mrs. McCraw drove off, I still had her knitting bag in my hand.

The thing is, we didn't do that, right? We didn't put her away. The Esther P. Marinoff will help her, right?

•   •   •

When we get back, I tromp up the stairs to our apartment wondering if Theresa's family has a radio that works. Then I see the note hanging from our door.

Cam,
  Send your boy up to talk to me at 1700 today.
    Warden Williams

"The warden?" I croak.

My dad takes the note out of my hand. "Looks like it," he says.

"Couldn't I do this tomorrow?"

"When the warden says jump," my father says, "you ask, how high?"

"Dad, we gotta talk."

"Give me a little time to rest, then we'll play ball, then you'll go." He winks at me.

I don't remember ever seeing him look so tired. The extra guard duty shifts are killing him. It's too much work and being a prison guard is the exact wrong job for him. He's too nice. My mother would make a much better jailer than my father.

I've just finished my book when my father comes out of his room with his glove and the ball in his hand. My mother is still sleeping. He closes the door as quietly as he can. "Dock?" he asks.

"Yep." I search for my glove. It's not in my room, maybe it's in Natalie's. Lately she's decided the glove is hers.

The door to Nat's room is closed. I can't bring myself to open it. I glance back at my dad.

"I'll get it," he whispers.

From the doorway, I see Nat's soft purple blanket in a tangled heap. Why didn't my mom pack it? How will Nat go to sleep without it? I feel like marching into my parents' room and shaking my mom. How could you send her to that place without her blanket?

My dad finds the glove on a crate by her bed. He puts it under his arm and heads for the door.

"Dad? What about her blanket? What if she needs it?"

"I think your mom was worried it would get lost." He presses his lips together so hard, they go white.

Neither of us says anything as we walk down the stairs. The dock smells like sardines and it's pretty deserted—unless you count the birds, which I don't because it makes me think about Natalie.

We decide to throw parallel to 64 building, where we live. This way, if somebody misses, we aren't as likely to lose the ball in the bay or bust out any apartment windows. The gulls scatter to the dock posts and wood pilings at the water's edge. They sit watching us like fans.

It's so nice to have my dad again. I was angry at him for looking for a job up here and angry all over again when he found one. I've been angry at my mom for making us do this, and at Pete and all my friends at home because I had to move and they didn't. I've been mad at everyone except Natalie. I always try really hard not to get angry at her.

Once, when I was little, I yelled at her for smashing a dugout I'd constructed out of cardboard and my mom didn't speak to me for a month. My father told me having Natalie as a sister is like playing ball when you're 100 times better than your opponent. You'll always win, but it will make you feel like a louse. I didn't see what that had to do with my sister ruining my stuff and my mother going mute. But it was pretty clear that getting mad at Natalie was the one thing that would never be forgiven.

My dad's not a great ballplayer, but he's a lot of fun to throw with because he's always trying something tricky. He sends a high ball I have to run like crazy for, then a fast glove-pelting stinger, then a low burner. I know all his tricks.

After a few minutes, when my arm is good and loose, I start talking. "So," I ask, "how long we here?"

My dad catches the ball and walks up closer so we don't have to shout. "We live here now, Moose, you know that."

"But what if I don't want to live here."

He shrugs. "Nobody wants to come to Alcatraz. But at least you don't have a number printed on your back and no bracelets either."

"Bracelets?"

"Handcuffs."

"Oh." I send him an easy ball with a high arc. "Natalie doesn't like it either. She doesn't like it one bit," I say, although I know this is a cheap shot.

My father catches the ball and waits a beat before returning a stinger. I'm surprised how hard and fast it is. It stings my hand through my glove. "If you want to talk about yourself, that's fine. But I'm not going to discuss your sister."

"Does the warden know?"

"Does the warden know what?"

"About Natalie."

"Of course."

"What's he want to talk to *me* about, then?"

"Just wants to meet you is my guess. It's decent of him to take the time to talk to you, Moose."

"Have you met his daughter?"

"Piper, yes. Seems like quite a nice young lady."

I blow air out of my mouth and roll my eyes.

He laughs. "The pretty ones are always trouble, Moose, but I think you can handle her." He winks at me.

"She told me she was going to tell the warden about Natalie."

"Like I said, he already knows."

"She wasn't nice," I say.

"Sounds to me like she was just trying to help out her dad. No crime there."

"Tell me again why we can't go home?"

"We saw where that was going, Moose. Natalie sitting on Gram's back step counting her buttons day after day. We wanted to see—just see—if there was another way. This school has skilled teachers working with these kids around the clock. It's an impressive place."

The gulls are starting to edge closer now. I stamp my foot and they scatter.

"You saw how she was when we left."

"Change is hard. It's hard for you, it's hard for me, it's murder on your sister." His voice breaks.

"You heard her screaming, Dad—"

My dad's hands go up to block my words. "Look, son," he interrupts, "I can't talk about this anymore."

"I want to know for certain this is going to work out."

My dad sighs. He looks out at the water to where they're

building the Bay Bridge—two toothpicks held together by a thread of steel. He's quiet for a long time. "Nobody knows how things will turn out, that's why they go ahead and play the game, Moose. You give it your all and sometimes amazing things happen, but it's hardly ever what you expect.

"Now"—he checks his watch—"you can't go see the warden looking like that. Go put on a clean shirt."

"I don't have one."

"Clean*er* then. We don't put the laundry out until Wednesday. Comes back Monday."

"Mom doesn't have to do it?"

He shakes his head. "The convicts do the washing here."

"The convicts wash my shirts, as in murderer convicts and kidnapper convicts, and then *I'm* supposed to wear them?"

He laughs.

"They darn socks too?"

"Yes, as a matter of fact. Do a better job than your mom too. Though don't you dare tell her I said that."

"Murderers outsew my mother?"

"Apparently so." My dad laughs.

6. SUCKER

■ ■

Same day—Sunday, January 6, 1935

I'm walking by the cell house now. Row after row of dark barred windows, all spooky quiet. What goes on in there?

I know the convicts aren't allowed to talk, but how could some 300 men not make more sound? Just breathing makes noise, you know. And all those windows? The cons don't sit around watching us . . . do they?

Across the road from the cell house is a fancy mansion with flowerpots on the steps and curtains in the windows. The only thing missing from the house is a lawn and a tree. That's the only tip this is Alcatraz. There's nothing but cement clear up to the door. Even so, it's strange how one side of the road is so different from the other—high society on the left, grim and grisly on the right. But somehow this seems like the perfect place for Piper.

I trip going up the steps and have to brush myself off and tuck my shirt in again. I comb my hair with my hand, take a deep breath and ring the bell. The door opens a split second later and there is the warden rising to fill the doorway. "Young Mr. Flanagan," he says.

"Yes, sir," I say.

"Just making myself a cup of tea. Care to join me?"

"No, sir. I mean yes, sir, I want to join you, but no, sir, I don't like tea."

The warden nods. His eyes look me up and down. After a long minute, he gives up command of the entrance and motions me in. "My library is upstairs. The door's open. You go on ahead."

I take an uncertain step forward and peek in at the living room. The couches and chairs look perfect, like nobody's ever sat in them. It smells like ammonia and there's opera music playing somewhere. This is not the kind of house where you can burp freely and run around in your bare feet.

The warden's library is a big dark room with heavy red drapes drawn closed and floor-to-ceiling books—the kind of official volumes with thick indexes Natalie likes.

The warden comes in after me and closes the door. He sets his teacup on the desk, settles into a huge winged desk chair and begins to work.

"Sit down, Mr. Flanagan," he says without looking up from his ledger. He sounds annoyed, like I've flunked his first test.

I sit down, only my aim is a little off and I clonk myself on the wooden arm of the chair. "Ouch. I mean ouch, sir," I say.

His face gets red. His sharp eyes seem to poke into me. He leans back in his chair and opens his mouth to say something, but just as he does, someone knocks on the solid oak door. "Yes?" the warden calls. The latch slides open and there is Piper. Her hair is curled. Her dress is starched. She's wearing white short socks and shiny white shoes.

"Piper, did you want to sit in?" the warden asks, his big face shining.

"Yes, sir." She smiles sweetly.

"We'd be delighted. Wouldn't we, Mr. Flanagan?" the warden asks.

"Yes . . . sir." My throat closes around the words.

The warden doesn't seem to notice, beaming as he is at her. "Piper, you feel free to chime in, now."

"Yes, sir." Piper smiles. She doesn't look at me.

"When convicts first arrive on Alcatraz, I speak with them personally. Let them know what I expect. I don't usually talk to new civilians, but Piper felt I should make an exception in your case," the warden says.

Oh, swell. I'm getting the convicted-felon treatment.

I try to look only at the warden. Try not to notice Piper. But this seems impossible.

"Yes, sir," I say.

"I don't know what you did in Santa Monica, Mr. Flanagan, but children on Alcatraz follow the rules. Exactly. Precisely. Without exception. Isn't that right, Piper?"

"Yes, sir," she says.

"We're a small town here. A small town with a big jail. The track record of the convicts we have includes seventy-nine successful escapes, nineteen unsuccessful escapes and twenty-four escapes that were planned but not carried out. That's before these men came to Alcatraz, of course. We've made certain there will be no escapes here, but I don't fool myself. These convicts are the very best at what they do. They have twenty-four hours a day, seven days a week to figure out how to get out of here. These are men who have been tried and convicted of the most heinous crimes imaginable—terrible men with nothing but time on their hands."

He waits for this information to sink in.

All I can think about is how stupid this is. If the men are

that dangerous, why have women and children living on the island? I know my father says that in the event of a break the warden wants the guard corps within walking distance of the cell house. And I know that the Alcatraz apartments are cheap compared to the cost of apartments in San Francisco. Still, it seems like an incredibly stupid idea to me.

"Yes, sir," I say.

"I have a great deal of respect for your father, and since you're Cam's boy, I bet you have a lot to offer. I'm looking forward to getting to know you. But before that can happen, we have to make sure we understand each other."

"Yes, sir," I say.

"We have rules here. Laws you must obey or you could endanger yourself and everyone else on this island. Rule number one: There's no contact with the convicts. You see them on work detail down at the dock. On occasion they'll help a family move furniture or paint their quarters." He pulls open the curtains and there is the cell house. The little hairs on my neck stand up at the sight of it so close.

"But"—his voice goes low and hard—"they are accompanied by a guard at all times. You may not under any circumstances approach them or speak to them. Women are not to wear bathing suits, shorts or any attire that is anything but completely modest. Undergarments are not to be sent out with the laundry." He turns to Piper. "Cover your ears, young lady." He beckons me with his finger.

I walk up close and he whispers, "Some of these convicts have not seen a woman in ten or fifteen years. You're old enough to understand what that means, Mr. Flanagan."

"Yes, sir," I say, almost running back to my chair.

"You can never trust a con. Nobody came here for singing too loud in church. Do you know what the word *conniving* means?"

"Sneaky, tricky," I say.

"That's right. Remember that, Mr. Flanagan. Conniving men with no sense of right and wrong."

Oh, swell!

"Number two: Do not enter an area that is fenced off.

"Number three: No visitors unless you've made your request in writing one week prior to the visiting day.

"Number four: Do not speak to any outsiders about what goes on here. Don't go shooting your mouth off about Al Capone. You say his name and hordes of reporters come crawling out of the woodwork ready to write stories full of foolish lies, dangerous lies. Know anything about Capone, Mr. Flanagan?"

"He's a gangster from Chicago. Killed a lot of people on Valentine's Day."

"Al Capone was—some people say *is*—the most powerful underworld figure in the country. Here on Alcatraz he's a number like every other con. The point of this prison is to keep these showy criminals out of the limelight. If I find out you're running your mouth about Capone, I'll ship you back to where you came from so fast, it will make your head spin."

Would you please? I want to say. But then I think about my dad and how hard he's working so we can stay here.

The warden's eyes flicker. He seems to sense his words haven't had the desired effect. "I know you're going to want to give that sister of yours a chance at school."

"Please, sir, don't bring her into this," I say, looking down at the carpet.

I can feel the heat of his intense blue eyes watching me.

"Fair enough." He nods. "Number five: You must walk through the metal detector upon entering and leaving the island. No dogs, cats or pets of any kind. No play guns, ropes, metal pipes or anything that can be used as a weapon. No old hangers or nails or anything made of metal or glass goes out with your trash. These convicts can fashion weapons out of anything."

"Yes, sir," I say, the hairs on my arms so keen, I could pick up radio signals with them.

"Now, my daughter tells me she's introduced you to the other children here." He nods to Piper.

Your daughter hasn't done boo. Far as I can tell, she's a bald-faced liar, I want to yell.

"Is there anything I missed, sweetheart?"

"The school projects?"

"Oh, yes. Piper is a straight-A student," he says, pretending to whisper.

"Oh, Daddy." Piper blushes.

"Her mother and I are so proud. But sometimes keeping track of all the projects she has going is a challenge for her. Annie and Jimmy both go to St. Bridgette's, so you'll be the only other Alcatraz child attending Marina School with Piper, and she often needs help carrying her projects and whatnot to school. We were hoping, as a favor to us, you might be willing to help out."

Emergency alert! Emergency alert! Moose Flanagan played for a sucker right before his very eyes. "Yes, sir." My voice squeaks high like a rodent's. I glance sideways at Piper.

The warden's smile is kind. "If you have any problems at all, my door is always open."

"Yes, sir."

"That's it. Welcome to Alcatraz. You can see yourself out?"

"Yes, sir. Thank you, sir," I say.

"Bye, Moose! See you at school tomorrow." Piper waves like she is the sweetest girl next door. For a second I almost believe her. That's how good she is. And then I realize she *is* the girl next door . . . the girl next door to Al Capone.

7. BIG FOR SEVENTH GRADE

■ ■

Monday, January 7, 1935

Now I get to walk into a school where I don't know anyone. Correction. I don't know anyone except a piece of work named Piper. One enemy, the rest strangers . . . this is not good, for cripe's sakes, plus it's midyear, so everybody has made all the friends they want already. No one will need a friend except me.

Was this how Natalie felt on the way to the Esther P. Marinoff School? Maybe some big ladies will come along and drag me inside kicking and screaming too. Sometimes it seems easier to be Natalie. People force her to do stuff. I have to force myself.

I try to remember how I would have walked into a new class at home. I guess that's the problem right there, at home I never would have thought about how to walk into a stupid room. I would have just done it. I take a deep breath and shove open the door.

Everyone is looking up at the teacher, including Piper. Third row, second seat.

The teacher is writing on the chalkboard in perfect Palmer method handwriting. I spot an empty seat and I wonder if I can get away with just sitting down like I've been here all year. The teacher turns around. She's got black, black hair and a tight white little face, as if her skin's a size too small. "And you are?" she asks.

"Matthew Flanagan. But everybody calls me Moose."

"I'm Miss Bimp," she says, looking at her roll sheet. Her pencil moves down the list. "Excuse me, Mr. Flanagan, but I don't see your name here. Are you certain you have the right class? Seventh-grade advanced English?"

"Yes, ma'am," I say.

She squints at me. "Big for seventh grade, aren't you, Mr. Flanagan?"

"Yes, ma'am."

Miss Bimp clears her throat. She puts her hand to her mouth and speaks behind it. "This wouldn't be your second time round in seventh grade, would it?"

Piper laughs first, then the whole class busts up.

My face burns. My ears are like two heaters attached to my head. "No, ma'am," I say.

"That's enough, class. All right, fine, Mr. Flanagan. Take a seat there in the back so you don't block anyone's view of the board. This week we're continuing our unit on oral reports. I'd like you each to write an outline for a two-minute speech. Remember, beginning, middle, end. Keep it short. Moose, have you written outlines before?"

"Yes, ma'am," I say.

"Excellent." Her stiff mouth flips up. This is supposed to be a smile. It looks like it hurts.

"The topic for today's speech is"—she writes on the board—" 'What I Did Over Christmas Vacation.' I'll give you fifteen minutes. Then we'll start right here." She raps her knuckles on *my* row. That just figures, doesn't it?

I take out my notebook. It seems like I've hardly started

scribbling ideas when Miss Bimp booms, "Pens down. Listen up. Scout McIlvey, you're first!"

Scout has the kind of hair that grows up instead of down. He has a friendly smile and everything he does, he does quickly. I don't pay much attention to what he says, but when he walks back to his seat, I see he's got a baseball glove under his desk. Within seconds, I've dipped my pen in my inkwell. *Do you play ball?* I write.

The note travels up the row to Scout. Even Piper passes it up with no comment. After Scout reads it, he turns around and smiles at me. Then his head ducks down to write his response.

South Field, it says when it comes back. *After school today. We need players.—Scout.* His handwriting is big and wild. It takes up the whole backside.

I can't believe my luck! I'm about to write *What position do you play* when I see Piper walk up the aisle. She waits while Scout moves his books out of her way. Even after Scout's done moving them, she still waits like he hasn't moved them far enough, although he clearly has. Scout pushes the last little corner in and she sails past.

In front of the room, Piper still waits like she's not going to open her mouth until she has every single person's eyes on her. She doesn't have an apron on either, which wouldn't be strange except every other girl in this class does.

"I sang a solo for our convicts on Alcatraz. I sang 'Silent Night' for Al Capone, Machine Gun Kelly, Roy Gardner and the others. There were tryouts in early December and I was given the only solo spot. We walked around the outside of the cell house caroling, so I didn't actually see Capone *this* time, but I'm almost sure I heard him call out, 'Sweet as a songbird.' "

"No kidding," a fat kid says. "*The* Al Capone?"

Piper nods. "The very same."

"How do you know it was him?"

"I recognized his voice."

"You gotta be kidding," another kid mutters.

"Moose Flanagan lives on Alcatraz too." Piper smiles at me like we are best friends. "Maybe he can tell you more."

What the heck was that? Take the little policewoman off Alcatraz and she runs her mouth like crazy. Capone this. Capone that. Exactly what the warden said never to do. And now if I don't talk about Alcatraz, I'll look like a chump. And if I do, she'll tell Daddy on me. Score one for Daddy's little miss.

The girl who comes after Piper is up front now, but everybody is so busy talking, no one notices. Miss Bimp raps her pointer stick so hard, she practically breaks it before people settle down.

The girl's turn goes lickety-split and so does the next guy's. I'm up now. I look out at the strange faces. My arms feel too long. I try crossing them, putting my hands in my pockets, holding one arm with the other. My pants are too tight in the waist and in the crotch too. How come I never noticed this before?

"My dad is the electrician on Alcatraz. I moved there, I mean here, from Santa Monica and the most exciting thing that happened to me this vacation was my mom didn't feel like cooking because our pans were still packed, so my dad brought home a plate of roast chicken, potatoes and cooked carrots . . ." I pause a minute. This wasn't what I wrote in my outline. I'm going free-form now. " . . . from *the cell house kitchen*. It was cooked by a kidnapper, a two-time murderer and a postal robber too!"

"Wow!" somebody says. "Were you scared?"

"No." I make a scoffing noise like this is the silliest thing I ever heard. The truth is I was terrified. For the first time in my whole life I skipped supper. Told my parents I had a stomachache, which has never stopped me from eating before.

"He could have been killed," Piper says in a stage voice. She's shaking her head as if it's a wonder I'm here to tell this story.

"They tried to poison you?" a girl with chipmunk cheeks asks.

"No, but they could have."

"Any of us could be poisoned at any time," Piper agrees.

"Is that all, Mr. Flanagan?" Miss Bimp cuts in, tapping her pencil on the desk.

"Yes, ma'am," I say.

When I get back to my seat, I trip on a girl's foot and knock my inkwell over. Ink seeps through a crack and drips on my leg. I spend the rest of class trying to clean it up.

After the bell rings, I catch up with Piper in the hall outside. "I thought we weren't supposed to talk about Alcatraz," I say.

"Why did you, then?" Piper asks, shifting her books to her other arm.

I open my mouth to answer but no words come out. Why did I, anyway? "Because you did," I finally spit out.

"Because I did? Isn't that the sweetest thing?" Piper smiles at me.

I hurry to keep up with her. Piper is a good six inches shorter than I am, but walks faster. How can this be?

She stops and looks at my pants.

I look down at myself and see a big black ink blotch the shape of Florida uncomfortably close to my fly.

"So, are you going to help me with my project or not?" she asks.

"What project?"

"Didn't I tell you? We're going to sell the Alcatraz laundry service to kids at school. You know, get your clothes cleaned by famous Alcatraz convicts Al Capone, Machine Gun Kelly and Roy Gardner. We'll charge five cents a shirt. No IOUs. Money will be split four ways. Jimmy and Annie will help us put the laundry through in their families' bags, so they each get a cut, plus you and I."

"You're going to sell the Alcatraz laundry service? Why?" I ask.

"I just told you why. Money." Piper starts walking again.

"Does your dad know about this?"

She snorts. "Not hardly," she says, taking off again.

"Hey." I hurry after her as she ducks into a doorway. "I didn't say—"

"Get out of here, you big baboon! This is the *girls'* bathroom," a blonde with angry pop-out eyes shouts. Three girls are putting on lipstick. Another is closing the stall door.

All the way to my next class I hear the sound of Piper's laugh. It plays over and over in my head.

8. PRISON GUY PLAYS BALL

▪ ▪

Same day—Monday, January 7, 1935

After school, I head for South Field, thinking about Piper. What is it about her, anyway? There were plenty of annoying people at home. I stayed away from them. It's living on a stupid island. It's like a prison. Okay, it is a prison. There's the problem right there.

It's only a half day at school, which I'm hoping my mom doesn't know so she won't wonder why I'm late.

"Hey, look, it's the Alcatraz guy," says a kid I recognize from my class.

"Who let you out?" another asks as he warms up his pitch.

"I can't stay late or they lock the cell house door. Gotta watch out for that. Nobody's home late on Alcatraz. Nobody gets bad grades either or they chain you up," I say.

"So hey." Another kid walks over. "I heard what you said in Miss Bimp's about almost getting poisoned, and I was wondering. Do you eat supper with them murderers?"

"Only snacks. Snack time is with murderers. Suppertime is reserved for con men, counterfeiters and armed robbers."

Scout laughs.

"What about Capone?" another kid hollers. "You met him yet?"

"No, I haven't had the pleasure of making his acquaintance,"

I say, holding my nose so my voice comes out like my great-aunt Elizabeth's.

They all laugh now.

"Does your dad carry a gun?" Scout wants to know.

"Nope," I say.

"Does he come home with blood on his hands?"

"Nah," I say. "He washes up first. My mom makes him."

I borrow Scout's glove. "Just don't get any bullet holes in it or anything," Scout says as I start warming up with a kid named Stanford.

Everyone seems to already know that this guy named Del and Scout will be captains. They call us in and start picking players. They make their choices the way my dad moves cards around in his gin rummy hand. The only wild card is me. I figure I'll be last pick because no one knows how I play, but Scout picks me third on his side.

Del and Scout measure hands up the bat. Scout wins, so I head for the dugout. Scout pulls me aside. "Hey, Mr. Alcatraz, can you hit?" he whispers.

I shrug. "I don't stink or anything. But I'm better in the field."

"But you can hit, right?"

"Yeah, I can hit," I say.

"You're leadoff. I'm second. Stanford, you're third. Meeger, you're cleanup. We'll see where we are after that."

I pick up the bat and give it a swing. It's too light. No clobber to a bat like that and the swing is faster than I like. I get into my ready stance. My head clears. No Natalie. No Mom. No Alcatraz. There's nothing but me and the ball.

The ball comes at me slow. Wait for it, wait for it. I swing. The bat whistles through the air. The ball sails by.

"Strike one," the catcher calls.

Don't think. My coach at home always said, "You start thinking, you get your drawers all in a twist." I glance up to see a group of girls watching. I wonder if Piper will walk by. She has to go this way to get to the boat.

I swing the bat back to ready position. The pitcher does his prepitch dance. Take your time. Turn your hips to the ball. Meet it. Meet it. I watch it arc out. Hold.

"Ball one."

What an eye. I can't help sneaking a smile at Scout.

But the pitcher's antsy now. He's ready to go. I swing my bat to ready and wait. The ball comes close. Too close. I hold.

"Strike two."

I stand up. "That was a ball. It almost hit me."

"It didn't though, did it, prison boy?" the curly-haired catcher says.

"It was a ball," I mutter. Doesn't this guy know the strike zone? Are we playing baseball or what? I nod to Scout, like he should watch the calls.

He seems to understand and positions himself behind the catcher.

The pitcher smiles. He wipes his hands on his shirt and sends a fastball. His best pitch yet.

It comes right where I like it, and I swing, but I forget about the bat being so light. I hit it, but not solid. It's a grounder. I drop the bat and thunder toward first base. The short stop fields and throws. The first baseman fumbles off to chase the short stop's bad throw. I'm almost . . . almost . . . I'm on. Not pretty, but I stick.

I look out at the girls. They're gone. They couldn't even wait to see if I got a hit? A wave of homesickness washes over me.

Scout's up now. He's a small guy. That's probably why the bat is light. It's his. He hits hard, though. Hard enough for me to take second and third. But then Daily and Meeger strike out and the next guy hits a pop fly the shortstop catches with his bare left hand. Del's team is up.

"What position?" Scout asks.

"First," I say.

He shakes his head. "Meeger plays first. How 'bout second?"

I shrug. I'm not wild about playing second, but when you're new, you're new. I borrow a glove from a kid on Del's team and make my way to second base.

First batter is pretty bad. Holds the bat like it has germs. Pitcher strikes him out.

Second batter looks like he's going to be good, but who knows, because the pitcher walks him. If he did that on purpose, then the guy must be really good.

Third batter wallops one hard right to me. I leap left and shag it on the fly, then rip it back to first. Meeger on first gets it in his glove and taps the guy as he slides back to first. Two outs! UNBELIEVABLE! My first double play ever! Not a double play combination like the famous Chicago Cubs' Tinker to Evers to Chance. But pretty darn close. I can't wait to tell my dad!

"Nice," Scout calls.

I try to nod like this is no big deal, but I can't get the grin off my face. Every guy on our team is looking at me and Meeger.

"Nice going," I tell Meeger.

"Prison guy can field them balls," Stanford says.

"Them gangsters taught him how to play," another guy agrees.

There's nothing like a double play to make yourself a friend or two. Maybe it won't be so bad here. Not so bad at all.

When it's time to go home, we're winning, 3–2. Scout tells me they play every Monday. I can hardly wait till next week. I don't even care if my mom gets mad at me for coming home late. I don't care about anything except playing ball again.

9. NICE LITTLE CHURCH BOY

■ ■

Same day—Monday, January 7, 1935

Theresa is waiting outside the door when I get back to our new place. "Where have you been? We're late!"

"Late? Late for what?"

Theresa sighs long and loud, like this isn't even worth answering. "You have a note from your mom." She hands it to me.

It says, *Dear Moose, I've gone to Bea Trixle's to get a perm. Make sure to get your dad up at six o'clock. We're going to the Officers' Club for a party at 6:30.*

"There's a beauty parlor *here*?" I ask Theresa.

"Nah, Bea does perms in her kitchen. But there's a barbershop for the cons in the cell house. Come on!"

I dump my stuff inside. "What are we late for?" I ask.

"We're going to the parade grounds to meet my brother, Jimmy, Annie and Piper."

"Wait, wait, wait! This Jimmy guy's your brother? How come you didn't tell me you had a brother?"

Theresa cocks her head and looks at me cross-eyed. "Because."

"Because why?"

"Then you'd play with him instead of me."

"He's *my* age?"

She nods.

"So why are you telling me now?"

"Now I know you like me."

"I do not."

"Yes, you do." She nods, her whole face earnest.

I can't help smiling at this. "If we're meeting your brother, I need my glove." I race to my room to get my old glove for him, my new glove for me and my baseball.

"Hah!" Theresa says when I come back. "Jimmy can't throw worth beans."

"We'll see about that," I say as we head back around 64 building, then follow the curve of the hill to an open cement area big enough to park thirty cars. There are lots of gulls here. Cranky ones too. Gulls are not happy birds.

A big girl with yellow hair sits on the wood side of the sandbox and a boy huddles over something. The boy looks like Theresa. Same curly black hair. Same slight build.

"Hi!" I say. I ignore the girl—Annie, I guess—she has her nose sideways to her homework like she sees better out of one eye than the other.

"Hey, Moose? I'm Jimmy," Jimmy says. He smiles quick up at me, then hunches back over an elaborate machine made of rocks, marbles, sticks and rubber bands.

"What is that?" I ask.

"It's a marble-shooting machine. Want to see?"

"Sure," I say.

He fires a marble with a rubber band. It rolls under a plank and onto a miniature diving board that plunks down and hits another marble that is supposed to jump a stick, only it doesn't.

"Shucks," Jimmy says, his head low over his contraption

again. He fiddles some more and then fires the marble again. This time it makes the jump. He grins big.

"Nice. You want to throw some balls?" I offer him my glove.

"Sure." He puts the glove on and runs back, his eyes still on his marble machine. He throws the ball the complete wrong direction. I chase it down and toss it back. It hits his glove and plops out. He runs after it and throws again. This time down the side of the hill.

"I'll get it." I cut down the path to the terrace below, where the ball is caught in the prickly thistle of a blackberry bush.

When I get back up to the parade grounds, Jimmy is at work on his machine and Theresa has my extra glove. "My turn," she says.

I throw the ball easy to Theresa. She wraps her arms around it like she's hugging herself. The ball falls through her arms. She chases it down, then throws with both hands from ground level, sending the ball willy-nilly skyward.

"I guess baseball isn't the Mattaman family sport," I say under my breath.

Theresa hands me back my glove. "There's something else I haven't told you."

"Oh, really? And what is that?" I edge away from her so I can play catch with myself.

"My mom has to keep her feet up. She's due to have my baby soon."

"It isn't your baby!" Jimmy calls, balancing a stick on two rocks.

"She has to keep her feet up, otherwise the baby might slip out all of a sudden and bump his head," Theresa says.

"Theresa . . ." Jimmy looks up from his project. He groans and rolls his eyes.

"It depends on how long the American cord is. . . ." Theresa's little gnome face scrunches up like she's thinking hard about this. "And how tall the mom is. . . ."

"Umbilical cord. And shut up about Mom's privates, Theresa!" Jimmy orders.

I look for a second at Annie. Something about the way she's concentrating makes me think she's paying more attention to us than to her work. "How do you do, Annie," I say in my most charming voice.

"Hello, Moose." She doesn't look up.

"You wouldn't want to play a little ball . . . would you?" I ask.

Slowly and deliberately she folds down a corner of her book and closes it. She snatches my extra glove and walks out clear to the basketball hoop.

I run up close. I don't want to embarrass her. She's only a girl, after all. I pop her one light and easy.

She catches it no problem and zips me a hard fastball.

"Wow!" I jump in the air, and I wave my hands around like some kind of idiot and then, before I can stop myself, I run up to this Annie girl and give her a big hug.

"No slobbering!" she cries.

"Sorry," I say, my face hot as a furnace. But then I see a slight little smile in the corner of her mouth.

"So, Annie." I walk up close so we can talk and throw at the same time. "Does anyone else here play?"

"No one except the cons. They play in the rec yard. Sometimes they hit one over the prison yard wall. The way they play, it's an automatic out. But when a ball comes over to our side, we get to keep it. They're pretty popular around here."

"If the cons don't want to hit 'em over, it must not happen that much," I say, catching Annie's brand of stinger, which has a little curve on it. Quite a good throw if you ask me.

"They try to hit them hard, but not hard enough to go over."

"Kinda tricky. How many you guys find?" I ask, winding up my own stinger.

Annie catches it, no problem. "I have one. Piper has one. Jimmy has one. None of the little kids do."

We're tossing the ball back and forth in a hard fast rhythm that feels great. My arm is purring. The ball, my glove, my arm are all working together like greased motor parts. Annie is so good, I don't hold back.

"Where is Piper, anyway?" I can't keep myself from asking.

"Charm school."

"Charm school? That's a laugh. Is it remedial charm or what?"

Annie catches the ball and holds it. She walks up close enough to whisper. "You got to get along with Piper. Otherwise she'll make trouble for you and your dad."

"Can she do that?"

"She can do anything she wants," she says, handing me back my glove, picking up her book and dusting it off. "I gotta go in."

"You going to that party tonight?" I ask.

"Everybody goes," Annie explains. She walks heavy, like she weighs two hundred pounds. She's sturdy, but not fat, and she has the best throwing arm I've ever seen on a girl. Pete would never believe it.

I look around for Theresa and Jimmy, but they're already inside. I toss the ball up in the air and catch it just as the four o'clock bell rings. On Alcatraz a bell rings every hour to remind the guards to count the cons and make sure no one's escaped. I'm about to go in when I spot Piper.

"Well, if it isn't our very own Babe Ruth."

She's being sarcastic, but to me this is the best compliment in the world. "I like to play. What's the matter with that?" I say, tossing the ball in the air and catching it bare-handed.

She looks around the parade grounds, then starts walking back to the road like I'm not the person she's looking for.

"Did you see me play after school?" Why am I asking this? I can feel my face heat up.

She snorts, but doesn't answer.

"They teach you how to make those sounds in charm school?" I'm half skipping to keep up with her, that's how fast she walks.

"They teach you how to be a nice little church boy in Santa Monica?"

"Oh, so now I'm a church boy? Talk about playing both sides and down the middle too."

"You won't help with our laundry service because you don't want to get in trouble. How do you spell Boy Scout?"

"I just don't feel like doing it."

"Right. I'll bet you don't feel like doing anything against the warden's rules."

"How do you know?"

She makes a strangled little sound in her throat and pulls open her front door.

"Why do you need me for this laundry plan of yours, anyway? Why do you care?"

"I can't put eighty shirts through in my laundry bag, now, can I? Annie and Jimmy will help, but that's not enough."

"How do you know I won't tell your dad?"

She rolls her eyes like this question is too stupid to bother answering and slams the door in my face.

10. NOT READY

Same day—Monday, January 7, 1935

Back home, I check the clock. Quarter to five. Still not time to wake my dad.

On my bed, I spread out two double ham sandwiches, a bowl of potato salad and the tail end of a salami and crack open my book. I've just finished Chapter Eleven when I hear the knock. Somewhere in the back of my head the knocking has been going on for some time. I run through the living room. Before I even open the door, I know who it is by the whistling, wheezing breathing.

"Mrs. Caconi," I say, staring out at the big woman framed against the green sea and the gloomy gray dusk.

"You losing your hearing, Moose? I've been banging on this door for five whole minutes," Mrs. Caconi hisses between breaths. "You folks got a call."

Mrs. Caconi is fat around the middle, with arms as big as thighs and bosoms like two jiggling watermelons. She is hot and out of breath from the walk up the stairs. But Mrs. Caconi is the one who answers the phone because it's right outside her door. Given her size and her difficulty with stairs, she seems the wrong person to live in the apartment next to the phone, but nobody asked me.

"Go on ahead," she wheezes, backing her big self against the wall so I can squeeze by.

I think about getting my dad. But he's been so tired, I don't have the heart to wake him early. There probably isn't time to get my mom and she won't want to go outside with all that stinky permanent goop on her hair.

At the foot of the stairs, I spot the receiver hanging down. "Hello, this is Matthew Flanagan," I say.

"Matthew? You are . . ." The male voice hesitates.

"Moose, sir. People call me Moose Flanagan."

"Oh, yes, Moose. We met yesterday. This is Mr. Purdy, the headmaster at the Esther P. Marinoff School where your sister, Natalie, is enrolled. Is your mom or dad available?"

"Not right now, sir."

Mr. Purdy sighs. "All right then, you'll need to give them a message. Natalie is not settling in as we had hoped. Tell them I'm terribly sorry, but as I explained to your mom, we were only taking her on a trial basis. They need to come and pick her up today . . . *tonight.*"

"Tonight? Is she okay?" I ask.

"Yes, yes, she's fine, son, perfectly fine. She's just not ready for the program we have here is all. Just not ready," he says. "Tell your mom and dad they must pick her up tonight. Can you do that for me, son?"

"Natalie isn't ready?" I ask. "But she's only been there one day."

"Thirty-six hours. Yes, yes, I know. These things become clear rather quickly, I'm afraid. Have your parents call me if they have questions. Otherwise, I will expect them this evening."

The phone clicks in my ear and the questions flood my brain. Why? What did she do? What happened? How could they know anything about Natalie in one day? They didn't even try.

I want to go back to Santa Monica, but not this way—not if it means giving this news to my mom. My feet feel suddenly too heavy. The stairs too steep.

I push open our door. My mom is back. Her dark hair is permed flat with one wiggly curl across her forehead. She's wearing a dress I've never seen before.

"How do I look?" She whirls around, her whole face radiant. I get a big whiff of sour perm and heavy perfume smell.

I open my mouth, but no words come out.

"I got my hair done. Didn't you see my note?"

"Mom." The words are frozen in my chest. "It's beautiful." My voice cracks.

My mom's eyes register that something is wrong. "Moose." She touches my shoulder. "It was hard to leave her there. Of course it was. What did we expect? But this is her chance, son. She's going to get better. I know it. I feel it right here." She pats her heart.

I can't look at her. "Time to wake Dad," I mutter.

The bed creaks when I sit down in my parents' dark room, but my dad doesn't stir. His hair seems to have slipped back on his head. It isn't growing thick and full across his forehead the way mine does. His bald spot, which used to be no bigger than a quarter, is now the size of a baseball. The creases in his face look deeper too.

I jiggle his arm. "Dad," I say, "we have to go pick up Natalie. Mr. Purdy called. They don't want her at the Esther P. Marinoff. She can't stay there, not even tonight."

My father opens his eyes. He looks as if he's just stepped on a nail. "Come again," he says.

By the time I finish explaining the second time, he's sitting up in bed.

"Does your mom know?"

I shake my head.

He takes a deep breath and lets it out with a whistle. His eyes focus on a worn spot on the rug.

"Okay, son. I'll take it from here," he says.

11. THE BEST IN THE COUNTRY

....

Same day—Monday, January 7, 1935

When my dad tells my mom, she seems to have no reaction. She goes in her room, puts on her regular clothes and comes out with her purse and her gloves in her hand. "Let's go," she says, her face blank, her eyes dead.

"Sit down, honey," my father says. "We don't have to go right this minute. Let's just take a deep breath here."

"NOW," my mom says, waiting like a child at the door.

My father's shoulders are hunched. He gets his shoes, jacket and hat and starts to open the door.

"No," my mother says. "You can't go. You have to be at work at eight. I'll go myself."

"You can't go by yourself."

"YES!" My mom shoves my dad hard. His arm bangs the wall.

My mouth falls open. I've never seen her do anything like this.

"Moose," my father asks, his voice quiet. "Will you go with your mother?"

On the boat, my mom seems better. Her eyes are angry now. Not dead. Here we go again, I think. Before the Esther P. Marinoff, the Barriman School was "It" and before that the heat treatments and before that the aluminum formula and before that UCLA.

At UCLA they made us cut Natalie's hair. Shaved it right off. They tested her like she was some kind of insect. They tested the movement of her eyes, the sensitivity of her ears, the color of her pee. They tested allergies, reflexes, muscle strength. Her speech in a dark room. Her reaction to Tchaikovsky. The way she ate, slept, burped, blew her nose and even what she thought. Especially what she thought. Nothing about her was private.

At home she'd spend hours in her room rocking like a boat in a terrible storm. But it was *UCLA,* my mother would remind us. When she said the name, it had a golden glow. They had promised us a cure, *if*—a word my mother can't ever seem to hear—Natalie's problem fit the diagnosis they were studying.

And so I spent months riding in the rumble seat of my gram's car to and from Westwood and hours sitting in the waiting room, until the day they let us know their findings. "An interesting case," they said. "But not what we're looking for. You should consider donating her brain to science when she dies."

"When she dies?" my mother said. "She's ten years old."

They shrugged their shoulders and handed my dad a bill.

Things fell apart at my house after that. Ants in the sink. Flies on the garbage. Cereal for supper. No clean dishes. Natalie in the same dirty dress. The blood of picked scabs on her arm.

It was months before my mother left the house again. And that was with my mom's sisters, my gram and grandpa, her friends and cousins all around.

I don't remember when my mom decided Natalie was going to stay ten. But I think it might have been then.

•   •   •

Sitting in Mr. Purdy's office, I imagine punching him in the nose. My arm twitches just thinking about it.

"I'm afraid," Mr. Purdy explains when he comes in, "she's more involved than we can handle right now. We're equipped for boys with the kind of challenges your daughter faces, but not girls. You might want to look into Deerham in Marin County." Mr. Purdy hands my mother a card with an address scribbled on it.

"Deerham?" My mother's voice catches. "Isn't that an asylum?"

"I don't think it's helpful to get caught up with words, Mrs. Flanagan. We're looking for a way to help your daughter. Let's not let words come between us."

My mother takes her green feathered hat off as if she's staying. "The kids who graduate from your school get jobs. They have lives."

"Some of them do get jobs, yes."

"That's what I want for Natalie."

"I understand that, Mrs. Flanagan, but it's not working out for her here."

"It's only been two days. Surely even a . . . *usual* child would have had some adjustment to a new setting. . . ."

Mr. Purdy grunts. Mr. Purdy is the kind of man who can make a grunt seem polite.

"My husband and I," my mom continues, "have done a lot of research on this and we believe this program—your program—is the best in the country. You are turning out kids who can function in the world."

"That's kind of you to say, but—"

"And I don't think"—my mother is unstoppable—"that we will be able to replicate your success elsewhere. So I wonder if there isn't some way we could make this work. . . ."

Mr. Purdy shakes his head. "She can't stay here now, but if you wish, I can put you in touch with someone who might be able to help Natalie. Help her . . ."

"Get ready?" my mother offers. She sits up straighter in her chair.

"Yes." Mr. Purdy smiles, his ladylike hands fingertip to fingertip. He tips them toward my mother like he's rolling a ball to her. Then he swivels in his squeaky chair to get a folder behind him. He copies a number down on a slip of paper and hands it to my mother. My mother looks at the page, then folds it closed. Mr. Purdy stands up, to signal the end of our meeting. I stand up too. My mother does not. Mr. Purdy and I sit down again.

I'm proud of my mother for this. Proud of her for getting all she can from this man, but I'm angry too. No matter what this little paper says, my mother will do it. Once she sent away for voodoo dolls and carefully followed the instructions some witch doctor in the West Indies wrote about how to relieve Natalie's condition. Another time she took Natalie to a church where everybody stood up and waved their arms. She read the Bible to her for two hours every day while Natalie sat staring at her right hand as if there were a movie playing on her palm and she couldn't bear to pull herself away. And then there was a school where my mom taught music classes for free until they let Natalie in. And when they did, Natalie just sat in the fancy classroom tearing bits of paper into tiny pieces. With Natalie, there never is a happy ending. But my mom won't ever believe that.

"Forgive me, Mr. Purdy, I'd like to know what happened," my mom says, her brown eyes staring him down.

"I had hoped Mr. Flanagan would be here with you." Mr. Purdy looks at me.

"My husband is working the evening shift."

"Of course." Mr. Purdy nods. He looks around his cluttered office as if he's searching for a way out. "Natalie is, I would say, unresponsive." He peeks at my mother to see if this will do. My mother doesn't blink.

"I'm afraid she . . . there was a bit of a skirmish over a box of buttons and some unfortunate behavior. Your daughter is ten, you said, Mrs. Flanagan?" Mr. Purdy's watery eyes are suddenly sharply focused on my mom.

"Yes," my mother says, her white-gloved fingers closed into a tight fist around the handle of her green pocketbook.

"She gets up early?"

"She likes to watch the sun rise," I say.

Mr. Purdy looks at me, then back at my mom. "As you can see, we are located in Presidio Heights. It's a fine residential neighborhood, but perhaps not an ideal spot for someone like your daughter . . ." His voice trails off.

My mother waits.

"And though our neighbors are largely encouraging of what we're trying to do here, we must be cautious about taking children who might strain the relationships we've worked so hard to build. Children who are, one might say, overly vocal."

"She screamed?" my mother asks.

"Yes, she did. For the better part of an hour, I'm afraid. Your daughter's voice is quite shrill, and coupled with her early-rising habits . . ."

"But you think this is something that"—my mother holds up the folded slip of paper—"Mrs. Kelly can help us with."

"Indeed I do," Mr. Purdy says, standing up again. He has his good-bye smile on and he's looking at his watch.

"And why is this different for boys?" she asks.

"The boys' cottage is located in the old maids' quarters, which is farther from the neighbors." Mr. Purdy sits down again. He sketches a quick map for us. It looks like a bad pirate's map with X's marked for the treasure.

"Did you take her buttons away?" I ask.

My mom looks at me, then back at Mr. Purdy.

"We can't have a child who screams like a banshee at five-fifteen in the morning in a neighborhood like this. Now, if you'd like to spend some time working with Mrs. Kelly, there's a good possibility she can help Natalie bring this problem under control. I can't promise you, of course, but if Mrs. Kelly feels that Natalie is ready for our program, we'll consider her application again in May."

My mother is up now, offering her hand to Mr. Purdy to shake. "Of course, my husband and I appreciate all the help you've given us."

In the waiting room Natalie's legs are open, the way my mother always tells her not to sit. She is seated on a needlepoint brocade chair and I see by the way her finger is moving that she is counting the stitches in the seat.

We wait until she finishes the last stitch at the bottom,

before she starts again with the first stitch at the top. Our timing is perfect. We've had a lot of practice at this, my mother and I. I grab the old brown suitcase that says NATALIE FLANAGAN on all six sides and we hustle Natalie out the door. She is walking behind us now, a teenage girl acting as if she's eight.

12. WHAT ABOUT THE ELECTRIC CHAIR?

∎∎∎

Tuesday, January 8, 1935

The next morning seems just like normal, with Natalie watching the sun rise and then asking for lemon cake. And my mom telling her she's a silly sweet pea and she can't have it. My mom has the little slip of paper Mr. Purdy gave her taped to the icebox door. Twice now she's asked my father how early he thinks she should call.

I hurry past the Mattamans' on the way down to the boat for school. The fog's in and everything is gray. The foghorns bellow deep low notes. First one end of the island. Then the other.

When I get to the Trixles', Theresa Mattaman sticks her head out. "Moose! Can I come with you?"

"To school?" I ask. "Don't you have kindergarten at the Caconis' apartment?"

Theresa ducks her head back inside. "Janet, I'm sorry. I have to go to school with Moose today!" I hear her yell. Janet is Bea Trixle's daughter. She is the same age as Theresa, but that is the one and only similarity they have.

"Mommy!" Janet whines. "Theresa's escaping *again*!"

"Theresa. You can't go out. I told your mommy I'd look after you, you know that!" I hear Bea Trixle call.

"Uhhh," Theresa groans. "When is my mom getting back

from the hospital? Having a baby couldn't possibly take this long. Do you think she went shopping?"

"Theresa!" Bea Trixle calls.

"Come get me as soon as you get home!" Theresa hisses, and ducks back inside.

When I get down to the *Frank M. Coxe*, Piper is there waiting for me. I've been so caught up with Natalie, I forgot all about Piper's "project." I wonder how long before she brings it up.

"Boys first," she says.

For a second I hesitate, wondering if she has the gangplank booby-trapped.

"You know, Moose, I owe you an apology." She clatters across the gangplank behind me.

"For what?" I ask, thinking of at least three hundred things she could be apologizing for.

"I shouldn't have made you meet with my dad. I was just worried about your sister is all. But now that she's safely off the island . . ."

What do I say to this? She's got to know Nat's back. My father told everyone when we didn't show up for the party at the Officers' Club, right?

"Oh," I say.

"Oh? Do you accept my apology or not?"

"I accept your apology."

"Okay," Piper says, "and I just wanted to explain something else too. Helping me with the laundry isn't against the warden's rules."

Here it comes. "Oh, really," I say.

"You bet," she says.

"All right. Let's ask your dad if it's okay," I say.

"Do you ask permission to put on your underwear every morning?"

"I'm just pointing out."

"I know exactly what you're pointing out. But no one here sticks to those stupid rules. You're the only one, Moose Flanagan."

I shrug.

"And besides that, you'll be going back on your word. You told my dad you'd help me. You promised."

"Why should I help you? You treat me like something stuck to the bottom of your shoe."

She smiles her most charming smile. "I'll be nice now."

"No, you won't."

"Well, for a little while, anyway."

I laugh. It sneaks out the corner of my mouth before I can stop it.

She laughs too. An icy wind blows her hair off her shoulders and bites through my sweater.

"Let's go inside," she says.

The boat pitches in the wake of a big ferry. I walk as if I've just learned how. Grasping the side of the door, I get myself inside the cabin, where it's warm and steamy like hot chocolate.

Piper's cheeks and the tip of her nose are rosy. Her long hair is blown every which way.

The cabin is empty except for two guards and a scrawny little man in a suit. The scrawny man is handcuffed to one of the guards. The hair on the back of my neck stands up.

"Oh, that's Weasel on his way to court," Piper says.

"What for?"

"Another appeal probably. He's one of those convicts that knows as much about the law as the lawyers do. They call them jailhouse lawyers. My dad says Weasel could convince the hens they're better off with a fox in charge. And then persuade the jury it was in the chickens' best interest to be eaten.

"You know, Annie would never do this if there was even the slightest chance she'd get in trouble for it." She's back to her plan now. "You don't know Annie. And neither would Jimmy. Not if it were *really* against the rules," Piper says.

I look at Weasel again. "Forget it, Piper."

"What if I promise to be nice to your sister? Will you then?" she asks.

"I'll think about it," I say.

"Well, think fast, because I'm doing it today."

"You'll be nice to Natalie, no matter what?"

"Promise swear to God," she says.

"Never call her names. Never tell your dad stuff about her. Treat her really kind."

"Double swear to God." She holds her hand up like someone's swearing her in.

I stare at her right through her pretty brown eyes. There's something true in those eyes and something false too. I nod. "All right."

"You'll help."

"I suppose," I say, careful not to look at Weasel again.

She rubs her hands together. "We're in business. All you need to do is talk about Alcatraz. Get people in the right mood. You'll talk up the place, kind of like the warm-up, and I'll tell a few people, then let the word spread. You must know some

Alcatraz stories," she says as the boat motor grinds beneath our feet.

Inside her notebook she shows me a small sign:

ONCE IN A LIFETIME OPPORTUNITY!
Get your clothes laundered by Al Capone
and other world-famous public enemies!
All clothes cleaned on Alcatraz
at the only laundry facility in the world
run by convicted felons including the notorious
Scarface Al and Machine Gun Kelly!
Only costs 5 cents.

I groan. "Al Capone?"

"It's only one little mention." She flashes her movie star smile.

"Nope. Not doing it."

She ignores this. We walk off the boat now, just behind Weasel and his guards.

"Follow my lead. Then, when I leave, you take over. That's all you have to do. Talk. Did the warden say talking was against the rules, Moose Man?"

"Talking about Capone is."

"Fine. Don't talk about him, then. . . . He's not the only convict we have, you know. Jeepers!"

In Miss Bimp's class, Piper moves into action. She motions

me to the back of the room, where history books are stacked waist high and a bunch of kids are copying answers for last night's homework. My head says don't follow her, but my feet walk back there.

"It's been a hard week, don't you think, Moose?" Piper says to me so loud, she clearly means to be overheard. "Did you see that *shiv?*"

"What's a shiv?" the girl asks.

"It's a dagger made of old silverware, or carved out of a pot handle. The cons use them to stab each other or kill *our dads,*" Piper says, though she barely looks at the girl, as if relaying this information is not her aim at all.

"I guess they found it in a library book," Piper says. "Pages carved out in a knife shape. . . . How did they find it? Do you know, Moose?"

I shrug.

"He knows, he just doesn't want to tell." Piper glares at me, then slips away.

"So, what happened?" the girl demands.

"Somebody got stabbed, I guess," I say.

"What's the inside of the cell house look like?" the fat kid asks.

"I've never been in there," I say, "but my dad says the cells are like cages. Each one has a toilet, a sink, a bed and a man."

"What about the electric chair? Anybody seen that?" a girl wants to know.

"We don't have one," I answer.

"How about them firing squads?" The fat kid is turned all the way around in his seat.

"This is the United States of America—we don't have firing squads," I explain.

"Yeah, that's not how we knock people off here. We fry 'em. I've read all about it. It's like this . . ." A skinny kid shakes all over to demonstrate.

"What about the metal bracelets . . . you know, handcuffs and whosey whatsits on their legs?"

"I think maybe they just wear them for, you know, special occasions," I explain. Out of the corner of my eye, I see Piper talking to Del. If he goes for this, everyone else will too.

"So, what happened?" Scout asks.

"With the shiv in the library book?" The girl seems proud of herself for knowing the word now.

"Like I said, somebody sliced up a guy. Maybe killed him." I have no idea what I'm talking about now. "That's the thing about the cell house library," I say, "it's a high-risk operation."

"Really?" a girl asks.

"Books are overdue," I explain, "they lock you up. They have a special cell for it. Overdue library book cell. If it's more than ten days overdue, they put you in the hole. Solitary confinement."

"No kidding?" the fat kid asks. I can see him fingering his library book, which I'm guessing is past due.

"Oh, yeah," I say. I'm starting to enjoy myself. "And you should see what happens when you forget to say please. Bread and water for an entire week. Forget thank you and it's even worse."

"Oh, come on!" somebody says.

"Forget to wash your hands before supper, they slap you in leg irons. Prison is a bad place, I'm telling you."

Scout is biting his lip, trying not to laugh. Most everyone knows I'm kidding, but one girl isn't too sure.

"On the other hand," I say, "we have the politest felons in America. They say please, thank you, pardon and excuse me. If you're going to be robbed or murdered, you really want a polite guy to do it. Somebody who offers you a chair and some milk and cookies first. It's kind of like being shot by your grandmother. Who wouldn't prefer that?"

"You must learn a lot living there," a skinny girl says. She's taking in my every word.

"Oh, yeah, on weekends there are special classes the cons teach us . . . you learn how to blow safes, make silencers, steal cars . . . thieves school, we call it. Homework's tough, though. Ever tried to get a dead body in a rumble seat?"

Everyone laughs. They all know I'm kidding now. Then the bell rings, thank God, because I'm out of stories. I look around and see Del has disappeared. He comes back a few minutes later with his sweater on but nothing but bare skin underneath. He rolls his shirt up and hands it to Piper, who is busy talking to Scout, sign in hand.

When we are all settled in our seats, Miss Bimp starts rattling on about the importance of good posture and how no cultivated lady or gentleman would dream of slumping during oral reports the way certain members of this class are doing. She is just getting warmed up when the notes start appearing.

How about tomorrow? one pencil-rolled scrap of paper asks.

No. Only today, Piper writes back in her back-slanted cursive.

How much for socks? another says.

Two cents, Piper writes back.

Will my blouse come back bloody? My mom will kill me if I ruin my blouse.

No.

Can you advance me a nickel?

No.

PLEASE! The note comes back again, this time written in pencil-grinding capital letters.

NO! Piper scribbles mercilessly.

When class ends, two lines form outside the bathrooms. One by one Miss Bimp's students come out, sweaters over bare chests, shoes with no socks, jumpers with no shirts beneath. I watch from a distance as they hand Piper their clothes and their money.

"Please, Piper, I can't take off my dress! Can't I bring something tomorrow?" Penelope begs Piper.

"I'm sorry," Piper explains. She rolls her lips together and shakes her head. "Our arrangements simply won't allow that kind of flexibility." She looks really sorry too, as if she would change the rules in a second if only she could. The girl marches off to the bathroom and returns, slip in hand.

"Can't do it. Too, you know, personal," Piper tells the girl whose face is now as red as her hair.

At the end of the day, I see two eighth-grade guys walking home bare-chested, shivering in the gray foggy afternoon. Piper limited her sales efforts to the seventh-grade class, but probably they had a friend in the seventh grade send their clothes in. I'll bet Piper got twice as many eighth-grade kids this way. I have to admit . . . Piper is pretty smart. But she's going to get in trouble for this, I just know it.

13. ONE-WOMAN COMMANDO UNIT

．．．．．．．．．．．．．．．．．．．．．．．．．．．．．．．．．．．．．

Wednesday, January 9, 1935

I hear something funny when I get up the next morning. And when I go outside, I find Piper stuffing extra clothes in our laundry bags.

"What are you doing?" I ask her.

"What does it look like? You won't help. What am I supposed to do?"

"You're just lucky that I caught you and not my mom or dad," I say. But as soon as this is out of my mouth, I'm sorry I said it. It sounds pretty lame.

"I'm lucky, huh." She smiles—so pleased with herself, she can hardly stand it. "I guess that means you won't tell."

My ears are hot. I feel big and stupid and I don't know what to say, so I go back inside, hoping someone else will catch her.

While I'm in the bathroom looking for my toothbrush, my mom corners me. "Moose, honey," she says, "I have some good news for you." She's smiling like she wants something. "Things are going to change around here." My mom takes a lock of hair that's supposed to be on one side of my part and puts it on the other.

"Mom!" I raise my eyebrows. Sometimes she needs reminding that I'm not five anymore.

She smiles and nods her head as if she understands she's made a mistake, then gives me a once-over. "Have you grown out of your trousers?"

I look down at my feet. A good four inches of sock are showing.

"Go put your other ones on. The brown ones," my mother says.

I go in my room, happy to have an excuse to put a door between us.

"I met with Carrie Kelly yesterday," my mother calls through the door.

"Oh."

"She says we need to do a clean sweep. Throw away Nat's button box. They'll be no more counting for her. No more obsessions."

My gut tightens. I come out with the brown corduroys on. "Mom." I squeeze the word out of my throat.

"Mrs. Kelly said we can't let ourselves get in Natalie's way. She said we're the stumbling block. If Natalie's going to change, we have to change first."

I blow air out of my mouth like I'm whistling with no sound. "So now it's *our* fault?"

"Moose," my mother insists. "You know what I mean."

"You only met with her once, Mom. Did she even meet Natalie?"

"Of course. She spent all afternoon with her," my mom says, and then natters on about how Nat's not supposed to count. Not supposed to rock. Not supposed to play with her buttons. Not supposed to do anything she actually likes to do.

"Yes, ma'am," I say, searching the medicine cabinet for my toothbrush. Then I figure out where it is . . . Natalie.

My mother follows me as I march into Natalie's room. Nat isn't here. My father has taken her out to the parade grounds to give my mom a break.

Yep, here's the toothbrush. Natalie has stacks of buttons in perfect lines all around it, like little soldiers guarding something precious. I reach for my toothbrush, but I can't make myself disturb her perfect button world.

"Well, actually . . ." My mother's voice has softened. There's a wheedle in it now. I freeze, my hand on Nat's door.

"This involves you. I've lined up some piano lessons to teach in the city. The warden is very well connected and he was kind enough to introduce me to a number of families who were looking for a piano teacher. We need the money, Moose. Carrie Kelly costs a small fortune and so does the Esther P. Marinoff, so . . . I'll need you to come straight home from school. I have to be on the four o'clock boat and that is probably cutting it too close. . . ." She shakes her head and bites her bottom lip.

"I'm supposed to watch Natalie?"

"Mrs. Kelly says you can take her with you wherever you go, just like any other sister."

This stops me. I face my mom. "Mom, nobody takes his sister with him everywhere he goes."

My mom's shoulders hunch down and a little excitement drains out of her face. "Well, they could," she says.

I stare at her. Suspicious now. "What do you mean, wherever I go?" I ask, waving the tooth powder at her.

"Wherever you go."

"Mom, it's dangerous. You're the one who's always telling me how—"

"That's what I mean." My mother is all excited again. I am back in the bathroom mixing the tooth powder and water in the palm of my hand. My mom has followed me. Her eyes are shining and she's smiling at the end of every sentence. "That's what's changing. Mrs. Kelly says this is just what Natalie needs. We need to help Natalie join the human race."

"Mom"—I brush my teeth with my finger—"we live on an island with 278 murderers, kidnappers, thieves . . . maybe this isn't the exact part of the human race we want her to join. . . ."

"Funny you should mention this, because I was talking to Bea Trixle about this yesterday, and you know what she said? She said we are so lucky to live here because Alcatraz is a lot safer than any neighborhood in San Francisco. She says she never locks her door. She never has to. Our bad guys are all locked up. You know how your dad's always saying the ratio of inmate to guard is three to one here compared to ten to one at San Quentin, which makes Alcatraz a much safer prison. And in the city . . ."

"Oh, great," I mutter as I make a cup with my hands and run water into it, then rinse the tooth powder out of my mouth. "It's safer than San Quentin, the second worst prison in the state."

"And in the city"—my mother says this louder, as if to drown out my comment—"Bea Trixle says those same criminals are out free."

"Does the warden even know Natalie's here, or does he still think she's at the Esther P. Marinoff?"

"Of course he knows, Moose. But that doesn't mean I want you to parade her around in front of him. I won't lie to you. He isn't wild about the idea of her living here."

"Then she should stay inside."

"Don't be silly. You don't need to hide. Go about your business like you would if Nat wasn't with you. Just don't go looking for the warden, all right?"

"Natalie doesn't know how to swim, Mom. What if she falls in?"

"Well, we do have to be careful of that. But I don't want you near the water either. Anything that's not safe for Natalie is not safe for you. So if you really think it's so dangerous here, Moose, then we should move back home."

"Good idea," I say, my voice low and hard.

"Moose!" My mother's eyes are like the lit end of a cigarette burning into me.

Then I remember. Baseball. "You don't really mean *every* day. . . ."

"Yes, I do."

"Well, I can't Monday. I'm playing ball after school."

She sighs. "I have lessons scheduled for Monday, Moose. But I have nothing for Tuesday. What do you say I try to keep that day free for you. . . ."

"Monday is when they play, Mom. Not Tuesday. Scout said."

"Well, ask this Scout person to play on Tuesday."

"I hardly know the guy. How am I supposed to get him to put together a whole game just for me?"

"Ask him. That's how," my mother says, and then softens. "Look, I know this isn't easy for you. I know you'd rather not have any responsibilities. But the fact is, you do. If you play baseball on Alcatraz, you can play every day."

"Almost no one plays here."

"Gram doesn't live down the street anymore, honey." My mom sighs. "We can't do this without you. Being around kids is good for Natalie. Mrs. Kelly says so. And if she's to get accepted in the Esther P. Marinoff . . ."

My mom is like a one-woman commando unit. She could win land battles, air battles, water battles, outer space battles too, probably. I wonder if there would be time to get Natalie and then get back to school in time to play ball with the guys. It would be embarrassing to have her there, but at least I could play.

"Could I take her to San Francisco?" I ask.

"No."

"Why not? You just said . . ."

"I just said it isn't safe there."

"It isn't safe there, but it's safe here, crammed right up close with America's worst criminals?"

"We've been through this already, Moose."

"How long will you be gone?" I ask.

"Even when I'm here, you'll need to take her outside with you, Moose. What kind of a kid experience is she going to have following me around?"

She can't mean this. Please someone tell me she didn't say this.

"Moose." My mother reaches for my chin again and tips my face toward her. "I need you. Your dad needs you and Natalie needs you most of all. Let's give this a try, shall we? Let's just see how it goes."

I pull my head away and walk toward my room. "What if I don't want to see how it goes? What if I've been seeing how it goes my whole life?" I whisper.

"Tuesday. See if Scout can play on Tuesday. Is that too much to ask?"

14. AL CAPONE'S BASEBALL

■■■■■■■■■■■■■■■■■■■■■■■■■■■■■■■■■■■■■■

Same day—Wednesday, January 9, 1935

I'm so mad at my mom, that's all I can think about. I don't care about whether Piper got caught or Jimmy or Annie had any trouble getting the extra clothes by their moms. I don't care about anything except figuring out how I'm going to get Scout to change the baseball day.

When I get to Miss Bimp's class, Scout's already in his seat. We chat for a minute, then I take a deep breath and blurt it out. "Do you think maybe we could get a game together for Tuesday after school, instead of Mondays?"

"We play Mondays," Scout says, working a hole in his ledger book with his pencil.

"Yeah, I know, but I can't come Mondays. . . . How about Tuesdays?"

"Do they lock you in on Mondays?" He laughs. I don't.

"My mom teaches piano. I got to go back to watch my sister." I leave out the part about my sister being older than me and nutty as a fruitcake.

He nods like he understands.

"Maybe we could play, you know, another game on Tuesdays. . . ." I say, trying again.

"Piper said they play ball on Alcatraz. The prisoners, I mean. Maybe you could play with them. Or better yet, get us both in the game." He smiles. His smile is the only part of him that doesn't move fast.

"We're not allowed."

"Oh, well, wouldn't want to play with them anyway. Probably steal all the bases."

I laugh.

"Think Capone plays?"

My throat tightens. Who knew not talking about Capone was going to be so hard? "I dunno," I say.

"I heard he plays first base. I'd like to see that. Do they let you, you know, watch?"

I shake my head. "Nope. But if the baseballs come flying over the prison wall, you get to keep 'em."

"Really? Al Capone's baseball?"

"I don't guess you'd know it was his."

"You have one?"

"Nope."

"Well, if you get one, I'd like to have a look-see. Beats getting my shirt washed, that's for sure."

"Yep." I smile at this.

"Anyway, I can't play next Tuesday. I gotta watch my kid sister and my two little brothers. But maybe Tuesday after next. It was fun playing with you. You were great on second. I'll try, okay?"

"Okay," I say. Miss Bimp is here now.

"You get a convict baseball, you'll show it to me first, right?" Scout whispers.

"Sure." I nod.

"Will I have to pay?"

"Nope. I get one, you'll see it free and clear," I say.

"You're all right, Moose." He smiles his warm slow smile and I scoot back to my seat.

15. LOOKING FOR SCARFACE

■ ■

Thursday, January 10, 1935

The next day it's hot out. It was like this at home in Santa Monica sometimes. In the middle of winter all of a sudden we'd get a summer day.

On the way home from school Annie told me we're meeting at the parade grounds, then we're going to head down to some secret spot where you can watch the convicts walk up to the cell house at four o'clock. Annie says they do this all the time, it isn't against the rules and sometimes they even see Capone.

When I get to our apartment, my mom's music bag and her hat are waiting at the door.

"I forgot to ask, what did Scout say yesterday?" she asks.

"He said he'd try."

"See." She smiles at me. "Was that so bad?"

Natalie paces back and forth in front of the window, digging at her collarbone with her chin.

My mom stops and looks at me. She seems to be thinking of saying something about this, but changes her mind. "Remember, just treat her like you would a normal sister. This isn't baby-sitting."

"Whatever you say, Mom," I say, watching Nat fuss with her clothes like something's too tight.

"What's the matter?" I ask Natalie.

"She's fine," my mother answers for her. "We've been all over. We've had a lovely day." My mom glances quickly at me and then away.

"She looks upset."

"It's just hot, that's all." My mom rubs her neck.

"She wants her buttons."

"Well . . . yes . . . ," my mom admits. "But I'm sure once you take her out, she'll forget all about it. Mrs. Kelly says it's just a matter of redirecting her attention." My mom's voice isn't quite so sure as her words are. She and Natalie have clearly had a hard time today.

"Don't you think it's kind of mean, taking her buttons away?"

My mom stares at the curtains. "We have to try this. You'll take good care of her?" she asks, her gloved hand on the door.

"Sure."

"I'll be back on the six-thirty," my mom says.

In my room, I dig through my drawer for my swim trunks. "Come on, Nat," I say.

Nat jumps up, motors to her room and shuts the door.

I knock, a hard rap-rap. "Natalie, let's go!"

She doesn't open the door.

I knock again, then push it open a crack. She's standing in her bathing suit.

"Oh, no!" I say. "You can't wear that!"

The warden was very clear about this. No girls are allowed to wear suits on account of the convicts. But how in the world do I explain this to Natalie? It's hot and she wants to wear her bathing suit. That's what we did at home.

"Natalie, you can't wear that."

"Hot," she says.

"Yeah, I know, but you can't wear your bathing suit. Put on something cool, but not that."

"HOT!" she shouts.

"Okay, okay, you're hot, I'm hot too."

"Moose cool. Moose bathing suit."

"You're a girl, Natalie. And it's . . . it's, you've got, you know, girl parts you have to keep covered up. It's not like home." How do I explain this to her?

"Moose cool!" she repeats.

There is no arguing with this.

Back in my room, I put on my corduroys again, which is like deciding to bake each of my legs. I find Nat's dress and hand it to her. She hands it back. "Moose hot. Natalie cool." She is almost smiling, her face full of victory. She's not about to change. She's not that crazy. I would laugh if it wasn't so frustrating. I don't want to miss the cons, because I'm curious, first off. But also because now I have to prove I'm not a goody-goody.

Nat fusses with the straps of her suit. "That doesn't look comfortable, Nat. Why don't you put on your blue dress? You always like your blue dress." I rub her dress against my cheek. "See? Soft."

I'm just thinking I'm wasting my breath when Natalie starts to take off her suit. I walk out of my room and close the door. "All done, Nat?" I ask when I hear her come out.

When I turn around she's standing in the living room, totally naked.

I can feel my whole face get red. Even the tips of my ears burn. I don't want to see my sister naked. "No! You can't do that!" I run to the front window and yank the drapes closed.

Now she's in the kitchen, lying on the cool floor. At least this is better. It isn't so bad from the back.

I think about the time we took Natalie to my cousin Cricket's wedding. It was boiling that day too, and right in the middle of the ceremony, Natalie took all her clothes off. But she wasn't so old. It wasn't like now.

The clock on the mantle is ticking. Three-fifteen. We're supposed to meet at three-thirty. It takes ten minutes to get to the west stairs on the parade grounds. I have five minutes to get out the door and a crazy naked sister on the floor. How does my mom get her dressed, anyway?

"You can take your buttons outside. But only if you wear your blue dress." I get the button box from where my mom has hidden it inside the radio cabinet. What else am I supposed to do? I shake the buttons down by her ear and try to pull the dress over her head. She doesn't take it off.

"You have to wear your underwear too. I won't look."

She doesn't move a muscle. Her bare skin looks so white against the floor.

"Come on, Nat," I plead.

"Swim," she says.

"You want to go swimming?"

"Natalie swimming."

"Okay. Here's what we'll do. If you wear your blue dress and your underwear, I'll take you swimming." I have no idea where I can take her swimming, but I'll worry about that later.

"Swim?"

"Blue dress, underwear. Swim later." I try to talk in her language.

"Moose double . . . ," she says.

"Double what?"

"Double swear."

I laugh. "Yeah, okay. I double swear."

Miraculously, she puts on her dress, her underwear, her socks and shoes, and we're out the door. Three-twenty-five. If we walk fast, we'll make it. But every time I turn around, Nat's stopped to rub her toe on the pavement. Then we have to count the birds. I try to get her to count *and* walk, but apparently this is impossible in Natalie-World.

I don't know what time it is when we walk across the parade grounds to the west stairwell. No one is there, but we can't be that late. I run down the stairs, leaving more and more distance between Nat and me. Then I hear them. I'm about to shout "Wait up" when Piper says, "Come on, Annie, I've lived around prisons my whole life, but I've never been inside the cell house. All we ever do is watch the cons walk up. Big deal. Don't you ever wonder what it's like in there? We got the biggest gangster in the whole world here. Don't you want to shake hands with Al Capone?"

The laundry plan isn't even finished and Piper's already hatching another? I can't believe her. I strain my ears, but I can't hear what Annie says back. Annie's voice is soft and sweet. Piper's is loud and scratchy.

"Al Capone . . . ," Piper says, and then I hear a stumbling sound behind me. It's Natalie. She's on her feet, but a bush is whapping back and forth like she just tripped over it.

"You okay?" I ask.

"What's that?" Annie says.

And then suddenly Annie and Piper appear. Piper makes a

gravelly sound with her throat. "What's she doing here?" Piper asks.

I try to change the subject. "Where are Theresa and Jimmy?"

"Didn't you hear? Mrs. Mattaman had a baby boy. Named him Rocky," Annie says. She wipes the sweat off her forehead. "They have a bunch of relatives over to see the new baby, and Theresa and Jimmy have to entertain their cousins."

Piper looks from me to Natalie and back again. "Can't your mom watch her?" she asks.

"She teaches piano lessons."

"How often?"

"Every day," I mutter, glancing back at Natalie, who is using her dress to fan herself. We all get a good look at her ruffled underwear. Thank goodness she put it on.

"She better not do that when the cons are around," Annie says.

"They can't actually see us, right?" I ask.

"Right," Piper says. "C'mon, they'll be up soon." The path is narrower here, so we go single file. Piper, then me, then Annie, then Nat.

I've never walked over here and suddenly it seems like a bad idea. I'm wondering if maybe I should turn around when I see a huge chain-link fence that blocks our path. The fence is maybe twelve or fourteen feet high with three strands of barbed wire run across the top. It goes up the hill, where it connects to the rec yard wall, and down the hill as far as I can see. Maybe even to the water, though I can't tell from here.

In the distance on the other side of the fence, I see the steps that lead up to the recreation yard. High up in the corner of the rec yard is a guard tower no bigger than a one-man ticket booth. I imagine there's a guard with a Browning automatic training his sights on the convicts, watching to make sure they don't pull any funny business.

"That where they go up?" I ask.

Piper doesn't answer. She's fiddling with the lock, a key in her hand. A big drop of sweat drips down my face. More drops follow and my legs go stiff. "You have the key?" My voice croaks.

Piper takes one look at me and snorts. "Of course."

"You can't see 'em very well unless you go close. We do this all the time," Annie says. Her voice is kind.

"But can't the convicts see you?"

"Nope. Not where we stand," Piper says. "But we gotta get in position before they come up the stairs. That's the important thing."

"You go ahead. I'll stay here." I try to make my voice strong and clear. "I can't take Natalie, you know, up there."

"Natalie . . . like she has anything to do with it. Chicken. *Bwahk, bwahk, bwahk.*" Piper clucks, flapping her arms. "C'mon, Annie." She spits in the bushes. "We're late."

I watch them until they disappear behind a bush.

"Would you get a load of that guy?" I hear Piper say.

"Ah, Piper. Give it a rest," Annie says.

Natalie and I settle on our side of the fence. I climb the hill to a spot that seems safe.

Nat is still standing up. "Nat, get down," I tell her.

Natalie's eyes pass over me, the way an electric fan moves on its course. But to my surprise she gets down. We settle in, huddled together on our bellies in the small space, which gives us good cover and a faraway view of the steps going up. I definitely don't want to be any closer. For once I'm actually glad Natalie's with me. Piper would have been ten times pushier if Nat hadn't been here. And Annie was clearly on my side.

We don't hear anything but birds chirping, the lap of the water against the shore and the revving of a boat I don't see. Sound is strange near the water. Sometimes faraway things sound close. And then I hear a dull steady pounding sound. Footsteps. Dozens of them. Then the first head pops into view. A dark gray officer's hat. And another, then white hats, denim shirts and pants. White hats, denim shirts and pants. I strain to make out faces, but we're much too far away.

"One of those guys has a big scar down the side of his face. That's Al Capone," I whisper to Natalie. I wonder if Piper and Annie are close enough to spot Capone. I wonder if they can see the 85 printed on his back.

The first guard stops at the top of the stairs. He steps aside and lets the prisoners pass one by one through the recreation yard door until only the guard is left. He takes one look down the steps and across to the industry buildings. Why's he doing that? Doesn't he already know they're all inside?

Nat is on her belly behind me, running her hand over the dirt, organizing it in little piles. She doesn't notice the men. She doesn't notice anything. She could be anywhere. Anywhere there's dirt.

16. CAPONE WASHED YOUR SHIRTS

▪ ▪

Monday, January 14, 1935

The next Monday I'm in a really grumpy mood on account of it's baseball day for everyone except me. I hardly notice putting on my first convict-washed shirt. It's only after I get it on I even remember. I take the shirt off and inspect it, but I don't find anything unusual. It's my shirt and it's clean and that's about it.

At breakfast my mom doesn't say anything about finding extra clothes in our bags. So either my mom hasn't put the laundry away yet or more likely Piper got them out before my mom saw them. Piper is quite the criminal.

When I get on the boat, there she is with three laundry bags. Then Jimmy and Annie pile on board, thumping their bags down by Piper.

Piper's on her hands and knees on the deck.

"What're you doing?" I ask.

"Too many to carry." She sits on one bag to smash the shirts down so she can add another stack on top. "Unless, of course, you'll help."

"How did you get 'em home?" I ask.

"As if you care."

"I was just wondering," I say when I notice Mr. Trixle dressed in civilian clothes. Day off, I guess. I sure wish my father would get a day off. But when I asked him about it, he said, "Criminals are criminals every day of the week. They don't take a day off, so I can't either."

"Why you bringing laundry to school?" Mr. Trixle asks without taking his cigarette out of his mouth.

"It's a science project," Piper explains. "We're comparing the weight of dry cloth to the weight of wet cloth."

"Clever." Mr. Trixle looks at Annie and Jimmy and me. "But I thought you kids went to different schools."

"Citywide project," Piper says. "All the seventh-grade science classes in San Francisco have to do it."

Mr. Trixle shakes his big head and takes a drag on his cigarette. "You got an answer for everything, don't you, Piper." He breathes the smoke out his nose. "Just like your old man."

Piper nods. "Yes, sir," she says.

When the boat docks at Fort Mason, Piper has the laundry in three fully stuffed bags. This is still too much for her to carry. It's not like she has dead bodies in there or anything. And I did promise the warden I'd help her. I pick up two bags and carry one under each arm.

Piper smiles at me, like she won. I pretend not to notice.

"Mr. Trixle didn't believe that story about the science project," I tell her.

"Didn't check the bags, did he?"

I shake my head.

"Well, then he couldn't have been that suspicious."

When we get to school, I wonder what she's going to do now. There's not enough time to give the clothes back before the bell. But apparently Piper already has this figured out. She walks right into the home economics room and unlocks the supply closet. Does this girl have keys to everything?

My plan is to stay away from her. I helped her get the stupid bags in, now I'm done. But at lunch when I see her in the cafeteria with the laundry bags, I find myself drifting over there.

"Moose! Moose! Guess what?" Scout calls as he runs through the cafeteria. "You got your Tuesday game! I traded baby-sitting with this kid in my neighborhood. Stanford can't make it. But everybody else is on!"

I thump my chest like an ape and smile so big, it feels like my face is splitting in two. "If you were a girl, I'd give you a big sloppy kiss," I say.

"Did my best, guy. I like to please the folks who bunk with criminals."

"Do you mind?" Piper barks. "I'm conducting business here."

"You get your shirt back, Scout?" I ask.

"Yep." He nods to me as Piper hands a neatly folded shirt to the fat kid, Deekman.

"Hey," Deekman says. "This is just clean."

"Yeah, so?" Piper says.

"No blood spatters. No bullet holes. Nothing?" another kid asks.

"Al Capone laundered that shirt," Piper says. "It's a collector's item."

"How do we know that?" Deekman asks.

A girl blows air out of her mouth. "It sure doesn't look like it!" she says.

"What did you expect?" Piper asks. She snatches the shirt out of her hands and holds it up so everyone can see. "Al

Capone's fingerprints are on that sleeve! The sweat of his brow dropped on this pocket."

Piper's clearly gone too far . . . now she's selling Al's sweat?

The girl inspects the shirt again. She shakes her head, her eye twitching.

"I didn't pay a nickel to have my blouse *washed*," says another girl, who had made Piper promise her blouse wouldn't come back with one single drop of blood on it.

"Yes, you did," I say.

Del cuts in front of the line. Nobody minds. In fact, they seem relieved, like they were waiting for him to take a stand. He plants his feet. "How do we know you didn't have your mom wash these?"

"Hey!" Scout says. "Don't talk to her that way. She told you Capone washed them, Capone washed them."

Piper beams at Scout.

"Here's your ticket. That's your proof," Piper says.

Del grabs the ticket. He reads it out loud. "Alcatraz Laundry Number 015032." Then he shows it to all of us. "That could have come off anything," he announces. "You could have picked it up off the ground!"

"Yeah, but I didn't," Piper says.

"Yeah, but you could have," Del says.

"Take it easy, Del," Scout says.

This seems to get Del's attention. He looks at Scout, then back at Piper. "I want my money back," he tells her.

"Sorry, no refunds," Piper says.

"I'm not doing this again, Piper," Del says. He's got the bulk of his big self in Piper's face. "I got better things to do with my nickels."

"Lucky thing too, because that was the one and only opportunity you'll ever have in your whole entire lifetime. You can tell your grandchildren about it," Piper says.

"Yeah, right," Del mutters. "I'll tell them about a brown-haired girl who took our whole seventh-grade class to the cleaners."

17. BASEBALL ON TUESDAY

■ ■

Same day—Monday, January 14, 1935

When my mom gets home that night, I don't mention Scout changed the day. I hate when she says "I told you so."

While I'm helping her clear the dishes after supper, Mrs. Caconi knocks on our door. "Phone call for you, Helen," Mrs. Caconi says.

"Who was it?" I ask when my mom gets back.

"The Beckers. They want to switch to Tuesdays now. Cotillion class has moved to Monday."

My stomach drops. I think I must have heard wrong. "So you told them you couldn't, right?"

"I did no such thing."

"I've got baseball Tuesday."

"I thought Monday was baseball day."

"It was, but then you said I had to change it, remember?"

"You didn't tell me Scout changed it. You said he'd try. I haven't heard one word about it since then."

This can't be happening. It can't be. "Can't you call them back?"

She shakes her head.

"But you said . . ."

"I'm sorry. I said I would if I could, but now I can't."

"Mom, you have to!"

"We need the money, Moose. If I get students, I have to take them. . . . Can't you play baseball here?"

"Can't someone else watch Natalie?"

"And pay for a baby-sitter? Even if we did have the money, how would we find someone who could handle her? We all have to help out, Moose. That's the only way this is going to work."

I go to my room and slam the door. But then I come out again. I'm not giving up.

"Mom, please."

She shakes her head no.

I go back to my room and sit on my squeaky bed, stewing and reading but mostly stewing. But being mad makes me hungry. I wait until I hear my mom go in the bathroom. Then, I make a dash for the kitchen to raid the icebox. My mom finishes up sooner than I expect and catches me with five slices of bread, a hunk of bologna and an entire package of cheese, plus one jar of mayo I'm holding with my chin.

"I'm sorry about the misunderstanding, but Bea Trixle said she's seen you playing catch with Annie. She said you two have a lot of fun. Can't you play with her?"

"That's different. It's not a game," I mutter.

"What about Natalie? You haven't tried playing ball with her in a long time. Maybe she'll surprise you," she says.

"And maybe chickens will sing and dance the polka," I mutter, pushing open the door of my room with my elbow.

"What did you say?"

I dump my load on the bed. "When's Dad coming home, anyway?"

"Midnight."

"He works all the time now," I say.

"I don't like it any better than you do."

"Baseball's just one day a week, Mom. Couldn't we work out something for *one day?*"

My mother doesn't answer. She goes in her room and closes the door.

18. NOT ON MY TEAM

....

Tuesday, January 15, 1935

Next morning Scout catches up to me before I even get to school.

"Hey, Moose, I've got six and six for sure, but I'm hoping for seven and seven." He talks like he can't get the words out fast enough. "There's a kid in eighth maybe, he's gonna try. He's pretty good, I played with him before. Where is your glove? If you didn't bring it, you can borrow mine," he says before I even have time to answer.

I look up at the blue sky and pray for a sudden storm or a big earthquake.

"Did your old team have uniforms? Hey, wouldn't that be something? Uniforms and everything, but how do we pay for them?"

I open my mouth to tell him, then I close it again. All day long I try, but the words won't come out. By the time the last bell rings, I still haven't managed to say anything. Maybe I just won't show up. Tell Scout I came down with a sudden case of the chicken pox. But that's a rotten thing to do. I'm not a liar and I'm not a rat.

Now Scout's outside of his French class, talking to Piper. Since when does he talk to Piper?

"Hey, Moose," Piper says. "Scout here has just been telling

me you're quite the baseball player. He says you're a lot more co-ordinated than you look."

"That's not what I said," Scout says.

"That's what you meant, though." Piper's long hair hangs in her slanty eyes. Her sweater is buttoned at the top and she has her gloves on.

"What do you want?" I ask.

"What do *I* want? Nothing. We were just chatting. Right, Scout?"

Scout nods. He smiles at her, then looks at me, then back at Piper. He shrugs. "She was telling me about those convict baseballs."

"Exactly." Piper smiles, pleased with herself. "By the way"—she lowers her voice—"we're divvying up the earnings at the dock tomorrow and you are getting exactly nothing."

" 'Bout time you gave Jimmy and Annie their cut. What you been doing with the money, anyway . . . laundering it?"

"Very funny," she says.

"I gotta go," Scout says. "Bye, Piper. Meet you there, Moose." He starts running, which is how he gets everywhere. I don't think he knows how to walk.

"Actually, I can't come today," I finally blurt out, my voice barely breaking a whisper.

Scout stops. He turns around. "What?" he asks.

"I can't exactly come today," I mutter.

Scout stares at me. Piper does too.

"Why not?"

"I gotta look after my sister."

"So? Get someone else to watch her. That's what I did."

I shake my head.

"Piper," Scout says, "will you watch Moose's little sister?"

Piper snorts. "Not hardly."

"Why not?"

Piper looks at me. She seems to be thinking what to say. "Because." She answers as if this explains it.

"Well, get somebody. I changed all of this for you, you know."

"I know," I squeak.

Scout makes a sound like he's in pain. "What about next Tuesday?"

"Can't then either." I stare out at the field where a line of girls are practicing archery in their white blouses and long plaid skirts.

"When can you play?"

"Lunch." The word croaks out of me. I can't look him in the eye.

"Lunch?" Scout shakes his head. He slams his book on the ground. Picks it up and slams it down again. "What am I supposed to tell everyone?"

"That I'm sorry."

"That you're sorry?" His mouth hangs open. He waits for me to say something.

There's nothing to say.

He picks up his book. "Fine. But don't expect to play on my team again."

I go home like I'm supposed to, but the second my mom leaves, I let Natalie get her buttons and I give her as much lemon cake as she wants. I'm not sorry about it either.

19. DADDY'S LITTLE MISS

....

Wednesday, January 16, 1935

The next day at school Scout treats me like a post made of cement. At lunch I don't even bother going to the cafeteria. I head for the library and eat by myself. Scout's the only real friend I've made so far and apparently I've lost him already.

When I get home, I write a letter to Pete. I'm searching for an envelope when Theresa knocks on the door. "Come on," she says, "Piper's giving out the money!"

"I'm not getting any," I tell her.

"Yeah, but we'll get candy."

"Candy?" Natalie asks.

"Annie will buy some at the store. And for sure she'll give us some. Now, come on. You can bring your buttons, Nat," Theresa says.

What else am I going to do . . . sit inside with Natalie all afternoon?

When we get down to the dock, Jimmy, Annie and Piper are already there. Nat gets right to work matching buttons to feathers to stones like this is her assignment.

"Natalie," Piper calls.

Deep in button mode, Natalie doesn't answer.

"Natalie," Piper tries again.

"What do you want with her?" I ask, sticking my face in Piper's face.

"Simmer down, buster. I'm just asking her to help me count."

"I don't think she's—" I start to say.

"Numbers Nat, we need you!" Theresa interrupts.

Natalie looks up.

Piper hands Nat the money, rolled up in a handkerchief. "Three dollars and twenty cents split four—excuse me." Piper looks at me. "Three ways."

"One dollar six cents, two cents left over." Natalie rocks with pleasure.

"Extra two cents goes to me," Piper says as Natalie counts out each share.

Annie and Jimmy discuss what they'll do with the money. A dollar and six cents buys a whole Italian dinner in North Beach plus a double feature at the movies or a month of swims at Fleishhaker's Pool or a bunch of rides on the streetcars—the dinkies, as Annie calls them.

I'm just wondering how much they get for Seals tickets when Mr. Trixle appears out of nowhere. Everyone freezes. Piper's money is put away. Annie's and Jimmy's piles are still out.

"Piper, Moose, Jimmy and Annie," he barks, "the warden wants to see you in his library."

Me? I didn't do anything. I form the words with my lips, but keep the sound inside.

Theresa takes off her roller skates, but then begins to cry because she can't find her shoes. Jimmy starts hollering at Theresa to shut up. A group of moms and toddlers who have overheard

Mr. Trixle's command stare at us, their mouths hanging open. Annie clutches her homework against her chest. She looks even paler than usual.

"You don't have to come," I tell Theresa. "He didn't call you."

"I have to come. Who's going to get you out of trouble?" Theresa says, walking in her two sock feet.

"I'm not in trouble. I didn't do anything," I say.

"He called your name," Theresa says, her whole face scrunched up. "Come on, Nat." She stoops down to Nat's level. "Moose's in trouble. We gotta go."

Natalie in the warden's office. My mom is going to love this!

"Leave your buttons," I tell Nat. She has most of them out now. If I wait for her to put them back, it will take hours.

"Yeah, Nat, we need you," Theresa says.

"Natalie help. One dollar, six cents. Two cents left." Nat nods to herself, following us. I shake my head in wonder. It's almost as if Nat's a part of our group.

We hike up the steep switchback road in silence. The wind blows the eucalyptus trees, a buoy clangs, a boat horn toots, Natalie drags her toes.

We climb the steps in Piper's house and file into the warden's library. The warden stares at each of us as we sit down. He says nothing for the longest time. The silence presses down on me. I didn't do anything. It wasn't me, I want to yell.

When he finally speaks, his voice is very low. "I am so disappointed. I can't even begin to tell you how disappointed I am."

Outside, the gulls are arguing. They sound loud, even

through the window. I glance down at Natalie, who is sitting on the floor, running her hand over the spines of the books.

The warden looks at each of us. He takes a pair of small gold spectacles out of his shirt pocket and flicks them open. Out of his pants pocket, he removes an envelope. All of his motions are slow and deliberate. He unfolds the letter and begins to read.

Dear Warden Williams,

My son, Del Junior, goes to school with your daughter, Piper Williams. On Tuesday, Del came home from school without his shirt.

When I asked him where it was, he said his shirt was to be laundered by the notorious gangster inmate Al Capone. Of course, I thought his imagination had the best of him. But when he explained the details of the operation, I began to see that the idea was simply too preposterous to have been made up.

It's bad enough that the great city of San Francisco should suffer the indignity of a maximum security federal penitentiary in its midst without being subject to these sorts of sick and dangerous shenanigans. I am appalled by the extremely poor taste and unseemly behavior of your daughter and her friends. I certainly hope you take greater care in monitoring the activities of your prisoners than you do in watching your own flesh and blood.

Out of courtesy to you and your long and distinguished association with my brother, Judge Thomas Thornboy, and the San Francisco Rotary Club, I am addressing this letter to you in confidence. But if I should hear anything of this *nature again, my next letter will go directly to the <u>San Francisco Chronicle</u> and the mayor's office, respectively.*

Thank you for your prompt attention to this matter.

Sincerely,

Mrs. Del S. Peabody III.

It's so silent in the room, I can hear the air go in and out of people's noses. Warden Williams folds his glasses and returns them to his jacket pocket.

"Let's start with some explanations. Annie Bomini?"

Annie's face is so red, it makes her eyebrows look almost white. Her shoulders are slumped and her leg is twitching. Her homework is still clutched against her chest like her arm is permanently stuck that way. "I didn't sell the shirts. I put them through with our laundry. It was Piper's idea."

The warden's eyebrows wag. He rolls his tongue over his teeth. "The one thing I've never had patience for is a person who blames someone else to lessen her own culpability. I can't tell you how disappointed I am to see you behave this way, young lady." The warden stares Annie down. "Piper speaks so highly of you."

"She's not usually like this, Daddy." Piper lowers her voice and steps closer to her father.

"Like what?" I ask. "She said the truth."

Jimmy stands up. "Yep," he says, and sits down again.

The warden looks like someone has poked a pick in his side. His hand shakes. He steadies himself on the bookshelf and then his eyes go cold and hard like something sealed in ice.

"Apparently I can't trust you children any more than I can

hardened criminals. Well, fine. I'll handle this like I would an uprising in the cell house. All of you will be punished without exception."

"Even me?" Theresa's voice is quavering.

"Theresa didn't do anything, sir," Jimmy mumbles.

"Neither did Moose," Theresa says.

"One dollar and six cents. One dollar and six cents. Two pennies left over," Natalie says.

"What?" The warden looks from Jimmy to Theresa to Natalie.

"Shh, Nat," I say.

"Two pennies left over. Two pennies left over," Natalie says like someone is arguing with her math.

"What is she talking about?" the warden roars.

"That's the amount left over," I say.

"Left over from what?"

"From what they earned," Theresa says in a tiny voice.

"EARNED?" the warden barks. "Don't tell me this is about *money! Money* changed hands in this shenanigan?"

No one says anything, but the quiet is clearly an answer. The warden looks at each of us. "Let's have it. Right here." He pounds his desk. "Every last cent."

Annie reaches in her pocket and pulls out her coins. Then Jimmy. Piper doesn't move.

Warden Williams looks at me.

"I didn't earn any money, sir," I say.

He glances at the pile of coins, mostly nickels.

"Why do you think they're locked up?" He cocks his head in the direction of the cell house. "Why do you suppose, Mr. Flanagan?"

"They, uh . . ." I swallow hard. "Broke the laws."

The warden ignores me. He waits. "That's right. Money motivated most of 'em. Is that how you want to end up?"

"No, sir," Annie and I say in unison.

"I wasn't born yesterday, you aren't the first kids to break rules, but you will be the last children on this island to ever do anything like this again. There is nothing about this to be proud of." He waves the letter in the air. "There may come a time in your life when you feel it's your moral authority to challenge a rule. But that's not what this is about. This is about greed and silliness and incredibly poor judgment. Do you have anything to say for yourself? Moose?"

"Sir, I didn't do anything. That's what I've been trying—"

"NO EXCUSES!" the warden roars so loud, even Natalie looks up.

"How about you, Annie?"

"No, sir."

"Jimmy?"

"No, sir."

"Theresa?"

"No, sir."

"If anything like this occurs again, all of your fathers will be dismissed without severance. Anybody know what severance is? Annie?"

"Fired without pay," Annie whispers.

"That's right, Annie," the warden says. He watches her. Tries to pull her eyes to his eyes, but she will not look at him. She stares at her hands.

"Shame on you," he says in a velvet quiet tone. "Shame on all of you. Annie, how do you think your mother's going to take this news? And for crying out loud, Jimmy, you think your family hasn't had enough trouble. You really want your dad to be out of a job with that brand-spanking-new baby? Do you know how hard it is to feed five mouths in this world? Any of you?"

Jimmy bites his lip. I can see the tears well up in him.

"Moose, I expect more from you than this."

He expects more from *me?* I didn't do anything.

"I've seen how nice you are with your sister. But then you get involved with something like this." He shakes his head. "I catch you doing anything . . . ANYTHING against the rules . . . I mean, you kids breathe wrong and you'll be asked to leave."

"Yes, sir," we all say.

The warden straightens his coat. It is straight already, but he does it anyway, as if the discussion rumpled him. "I'll be speaking to all of your parents about this. This money will be returned to your classmates. I will make those arrangements *myself.* Now get out of my sight, every one of you. And you, young lady." He nods to Piper without looking at her. "I'm not finished with you yet."

As we file out of the office, I see Piper lean over and whisper to her father like she's his buddy, not his daughter. The little slime. She'll get out of this. She will.

20. WARNING

■■■■■■■■■■■■■■■■■■■■■■■■■■■■■■■■■■■■

Same day—Wednesday, January 16, 1935

I feel bad for Jimmy and Annie. They're going to really get it. I won't, though. I'll explain what happened to my dad. He'll understand. He always does.

We head to the parade grounds, but when we get to the turnoff, Natalie keeps plowing down toward the dock. Her buttons are there. How could I forget? Without any discussion, we follow her down.

Theresa puts her skates on, but then just sits. Annie and I kick an old can around. Natalie picks up where she left off, matching buttons to feathers and stones. Jimmy begins building another machine. Every now and then he finds a rock he thinks Natalie might want and he puts it in a pile for her. Apparently he knows the kind she likes, because Natalie seems to give these stones a special place in her elaborate grid.

I spin around and smack the can backward just for the heck of it. I turn back to see it sail ninety degrees the wrong direction and land right in the middle of Nat's button box, tipping it into her grid game.

Natalie freezes.

I race over there. "I'm sorry, Nat, I'm so sorry." I kneel down, throw the can away and try to put the buttons back as fast as I can.

But it's too late. Nat sits motionless. No one can be still like Natalie. She's still like not even her blood is moving inside her.

"Nat, we can make them like they were. It will be fun! Come on." I pick up a smooth gray stone and try to think what Nat would match with this.

But Natalie doesn't look. She curls up into a tight little ball on the cement. Buttons, stones and feathers all around.

Annie and Jimmy are kneeling with me now.

"Nat," I say gently. "I'm sorry. We'll help you put them back. We'll make them just like before." A fly lands on her cheek. Natalie doesn't flinch. Annie shoos it away.

"Come on, Natalie, it's okay." Annie tries too. She makes her voice soothing and sweet.

But Natalie doesn't move.

"Nat, we'll be careful. It won't happen again. Look! Birds, nine birds!" I point to one lone gull pecking the ground.

But she doesn't look. And then Theresa skates over.

"Natalie," Theresa commands, "it's okay. *I'm* here now."

But Natalie has gone away somewhere deep inside. Only her body is left, rolled up tight and completely still.

Theresa and I put her buttons back as best we can, arguing over where they should go. Annie shoos flies from Natalie. Jimmy keeps on building his machine, though every few minutes he adds another stone to Natalie's pile.

We sit with her. Annie and Theresa, Jimmy and me. Keep her company wherever she's gone.

That is the way my mom finds us when she gets off the boat, her music bag over her shoulder.

"Moose!" My mother looks at Natalie and then me. "What happened? What's the matter?" She runs toward us.

"I don't know, Mom. We . . . I . . . tipped over her buttons."

"Why did you let her take them out?"

"I dunno. She wanted them."

"How long has she been like this?"

"Half an hour, maybe."

My mom kneels down. She strokes Nat's face gently, gently, and pushes the hair out of her eyes.

"Get them out of here." My mom spits the words out.

"Mom, it's—"

"I won't have her made a spectacle."

"It's really not like that. They like her," I say.

"NOW, Moose!"

"Annie, could you . . ." My mouth hangs open waiting for the rest of the sentence to come out.

Annie looks at my mom and Natalie. I see in Annie's small blue eyes that she understands. "Theresa, Jimmy, get a move on. We can't stay down here," Annie commands.

Theresa stamps her skate so hard, she bends the wheel. "That stinks! Why do *we* have to leave?" she says as Jimmy and Annie pull her up the hill.

I find my dad at the electrical shop. He carries Nat home and puts her in bed. At first she has her eyes open that weird way, but then pretty soon she closes them.

When my mom comes out of Nat's room, her face is as white as flour.

"Honey, you should lie down," my father says.

My mother nods and heads for her room.

"I don't know how much longer she can take this," my father says. I don't know if he means Natalie or my mother.

When Mr. Trixle knocks on the door, my mom and Natalie

are sound asleep. The set of Mr. Trixle's jaw and his formal, military nod makes me wish more than anything that I'd talked to my father about what happened with the warden before he heard it from someone else.

Too late. He and Mr. Trixle are out the door. When my dad comes back, he chomps his toothpicks hard and angry.

"Moose." He motions with his head like I should follow. We go down to the dock and around to the southern tip of the island past the sixteen-foot sign that says WARNING: PERSONS PROCURING OR CONCEALING ESCAPE OF PRISONERS ARE SUBJECT TO PROSECUTION AND IMPRISONMENT. Jagged lines of orange and pink carve up the sky.

My father throws a stone in the orange-tinted water. "Please tell me you didn't know anything about this," he says.

I open my mouth to explain how it wasn't me, then his words register in my brain. I close my mouth.

He closes his eyes and shakes his head.

"I didn't sell the laundry," I say. "I didn't get any money."

"But you knew about it."

"Yeah, but I'm not a—you don't want me to be a snitch, do you?"

"I don't want you to be a snitch? This isn't some schoolyard game. I almost lost my job here, Moose. Do you know what that means to us?"

I look out at the darkening sky. "If you lost your job, we could go home."

"Is that what you think? That we can waltz back home?" He snorts.

"We could live in our old house and you could work at Sam Jensen Electric like you have my whole life."

"Sam's got a new guy working for him, and some other family lives at 2828 B Montana Avenue. That isn't our life anymore. It isn't our home. We live here. And if I lose my job, who knows where we'll live. Check out the lines of men looking for work someday, Moose."

"Dad—"

"I will not hear what my own son is doing from Darby Trixle. Do you understand me? You know what I said to him? I said, 'Oh, no, Moose would never be involved with something like that. He would tell me.'"

"Well, I was going to, but then it was such a bad day today with Natalie—"

"I DON'T MEAN AFTER THE FACT, MOOSE." He stares at me. I stare at the dark ground. I've never seen my father like this.

"I want your bat, your ball and both your gloves. I'm going to keep them for a while. I haven't decided how long. And if anything like this happens again, that will be it for you and baseball."

"Dad, come on." The words crawl out of my throat.

"I won't have this."

"You're treating me like I did everything wrong. It's not fair."

"If you didn't know anything about this, it wouldn't be fair. But you knew all about it, and you didn't do anything to stop it."

"At home this never would have happened. At home I wasn't responsible for everyone else in the world."

"That's not what I'm saying and you know it."

"So I knew what Piper was doing. Okay? But that doesn't mean I did anything."

"Life isn't so cut and dried as you like to make it, Moose. You have to use your head."

"I used my head."

"I have to be able to depend on you. Can I count on you or not?" my dad asks.

I can't even nod. Can't move my head.

"Moose?"

"Yeah," I say.

"All right then," he says.

PART
TWO

21. It Never Rains on Monday

Thursday, March 28, 1935

The entire month of February and half of March, it rains. Drizzling rain, driving rain, lightning storms and thunder. Big fat sloppy drops, little misty ones and the kind that sting when they come down. It rains every darn stupid day, except baseball day. Monday after Monday dawns bright and clear like some kind of baseball spell. Every Monday I see Scout and them warming up on my way to the boat. I walk by without even looking.

On Alcatraz there's nothing to do, no one to do it with and nothing to look forward to either. I haven't even been thinking about Pete all that much. He isn't much of a letter writer and it doesn't look like I'll be going home anytime soon. Hard to keep up a friendship if you never hear from a person. Annie goes to church with her mom every day. I didn't know it was possible to go to church that much. Piper's off the island, living with her grandma on Nob Hill. Annie says that's because she got in trouble too. But Piper says it's because she's sick to death of us.

Mostly I'm glad she's gone. It makes everything easier. I don't even see her much at school now. She's got her own friends, and slowly, day by day, I have mine. Besides, who wants to talk to Piper? Every time I see her, she tells me how much fun she's having living in San Francisco. How irritating is that?

My dad gave me back my gloves and my baseball in the middle of February. But with no one to play with, it hasn't done me a whit of good. I tried one day to get some guys to play with me at lunch, but without Scout, they wouldn't.

Jimmy was the only one of us who didn't get in trouble. His mom was so busy with the new baby, I guess she forgot. Or maybe she knew him well enough to know it wasn't his idea. I still feel awful about the stuff with my dad. I can't stand that he thinks I let him down. But every time I try to talk to him about it, he says, "Water under the bridge, Moose. Let's move on."

The only thing that's saved me from going completely nuts is bowling. I never thought I'd care about bowling. You roll a ball and knock things over . . . what kind of a sport is that? But apparently I'm desperate, because whenever Theresa's mom doesn't need her to help with baby Rocky, we take Natalie down to the bowling alley in the Officers' Club. It's embarrassing to spend all your time with a seven-year-old girl, but Jimmy is always fiddling with his mechanical devices, so what am I supposed to do?

And then there's Natalie. She hasn't had a fit since the day we got in trouble with the warden more than two months ago now. Not one. And though I let her have her buttons or her rocks, or at the Officers' Club her toothpicks, she seems easier and more present.

I've met Mrs. Kelly now a couple of times. She's a short round ball of a woman with a sturdy build and hair the color of plumbing pipes. I didn't like the way she looked at me, as if she was trying to find something wrong. In fact, I overheard her telling my mom that sometimes there is more than one kid affected in the same family. "There's nothing wrong with me, you old coot!" I felt like screaming in her ear.

I didn't, of course. I'm always polite. But even my mother was upset at this comment. "Don't let Moose fool you," she said. "He's smarter than he looks."

What is it with me that even my own mother thinks I look stupid?

Another funny thing is how used to living on an island with a bunch of criminals I am. It would seem strange to live with regular people after this. Even when I saw the convicts unload the laundry from the boats, it was boring. Nothing to say about it, really. I got tired of watching after a minute or two.

And then finally, in late March, the weather broke. It got sunny and warm and there were wildflowers poking up through every crack in the cement. That's when Piper came back to Alcatraz to live and Annie's mom returned to their twice-a-week church schedule.

"Here comes trouble," my dad said when he saw Piper back.

He's right too. It's like the last two months haven't happened for her. Her head is full of just as many schemes as it was before.

On the way home from school today she called a meeting on the parade grounds. When Nat and I got there, I could already tell Piper was up to something.

"What is it?" I demand.

"I'm not telling until everyone's here."

"Nobody's going to do what you say anymore, you know. Nobody wants to get in trouble," I say.

"Nobody's going to get in trouble."

"That's what you said the last time."

"This isn't against the rules."

"You said that the last time too."

"Why is it I'm responsible for everything?" she asks as she waves to Theresa, Jimmy and Annie to hurry up.

I roll my eyes.

"Sunday," she announces when we're settled in our private spot at the top of the west stairs. "We've all got to be on the nine-thirty boat to the city and return on the ten."

"A round-trip? Why?" I ask.

"Al Capone's mama is coming to Alcatraz. She's scheduled for the ten A.M. run from Fort Mason." Piper shakes her head and sighs. "How did you survive here without me?"

"How do you know about this?" I ask.

"I have my ways," Piper says. She stuffs a stick of gum in her mouth, then shoves the pack back in her pocket without offering any of us a piece.

"Which are?" I ask.

"I read Al's mail. I get to read everything, even the stuff he doesn't get to see. He gets a lot of letters from people asking for money that my mom mails back. Cons are only supposed to get letters from relatives."

"How come your mom gets to do it?"

"My dad trusts her."

"Doesn't want Capone's business all over the street," I say.

Piper nods. "This morning I read a letter from Mae Capone—that's Al's wife." She looks at me as if I'm the only one who wouldn't know that. "She said Al's mama is scheduled to be on the boat March thirty-one, ten A.M. run." Piper has a big smug smile on her face. She's waiting for us to tell her how clever she is.

"Smart," Jimmy says.

Piper takes a bow.

"Thirty-first, ten A.M., thirty-first, ten A.M.," Natalie says.

"But we won't get in trouble for this?"

She shrugs. "We're allowed to take the boat whenever we want. What could we get in trouble for?"

I try to figure out how this could get us in trouble. I can't come up with anything. Nothing at all.

"I'm bringing Rocky," Theresa announces. "This is going to be history. He has to be there."

"What's past is always history, stupid," Jimmy says. "And you're not bringing Rocky. Mom will never let you."

"Where I go, he goes," Theresa announces.

"He's not here *now*, is he?" Jimmy asks.

"Hold it!" Piper commands, her palm raised high. "Jimmy's right, don't bring the baby. Annie, can you get out of church?"

Annie shakes her head. "I doubt it," she says.

Piper looks down. She rolls her tongue around in her mouth. "Could if you wanted to."

Annie's nostrils flare out. She says nothing.

"Moose, are you going to bring, you know . . ." Piper dips her head toward Natalie, who is sitting quietly dragging her fingers along a patch of moss. "No offense or anything"—Piper flashes her fake smile—"but I don't think you should."

"You know what? That's none of your business," I shoot back. I decide about Natalie. Not Piper.

22. AL CAPONE'S MAMA

■ ■

Sunday, March 31, 1935

When the nine-thirty boat pulls up, Piper is dressed for charm school: white gloves, white hat, pink sweater, pink hair ribbon.

"Where's Theresa?" I ask Jimmy as we clomp on board.

"Not coming," Jimmy says.

Theresa must have decided that if Rocky can't come, she's not going either. She's pretty possessive about him. It's almost as if she gave birth to that baby herself.

On the boat, we head straight for the front, where none of us usually stand. I want to be the first to see Al Capone's mom waiting at the dock at Fort Mason. When the boat starts moving, we lean against the rail, straining to see the city in the hazy morning. It's a while before we see much of anything, but finally we make out the dock and then little specks of color that seem like they are people. One of those dots is the mother of public enemy number one, I think when I hear a faint wailing behind me.

"What's that?" I ask Piper as the crying gets louder. And then out of the cabin comes Theresa carrying a howling baby wrapped in a blue crocheted blanket. Rocky's whole face is red like butcher meat. His cries are loud enough to make dogs go deaf.

"Jimmy! What's Rocky doing here?" Piper barks.

"Jimmy! Help me!" Theresa cries.

"How did you get on?" Jimmy asks. "Mom is going to kill you!"

"Who says she has to know?" Theresa whines. "Now calm him down." She shoves the screaming infant in his arms, which only makes Rocky cry even louder—though I wouldn't have thought this was possible.

"Mom walks him!" Theresa orders.

Jimmy tries walking Rocky up and down the rocking boat. He's a big baby and Jimmy doesn't seem to have a good grip.

"Don't drop him, Jimmy!" Theresa scrambles after him, trying to tuck his chubby little legs back in the blanket.

My gram once told me that babies love the gentle sway of cars and boats. But not Rocky. When the boat pulls up to the dock, that baby is crying so loudly, Mrs. Mattaman can probably hear him on Alcatraz.

In the small group of people waiting on the dock at Fort Mason, there's only one woman who could be Teresina Capone. She's the old Italian woman with a big ruddy face and white-gray wavy hair. Mrs. Capone has a thick build, round shoulders and dark old-fashioned lace-up clothing that looks hot and uncomfortable. I thought she'd be blonde, wearing expensive furs, or flashy like her son in a canary yellow cape. She looks like anyone's grandma.

As soon as Mrs. Capone comes on board, Piper claims the bench next to her and I sit behind them.

"Hello." Piper holds her hand out to Mrs. Capone. "My name is Piper Williams. Pleased to meet you."

Mrs. Capone ignores her. She reads a letter, which she holds so close to her face, it seems like it would make her cross-eyed.

I don't know if this is because she can't see well or because she's trying to keep its contents from prying eyes, but whatever the reason, it's an effective block.

"Excuse me!" Piper tries again. "EXCUSE ME!" She drops her small pink purse on Mrs. Capone's toe. "Oh, forgive me!" she cries.

Mrs. Capone looks down at her toe and then up at Piper in surprise. I hope Piper didn't have anything heavy in there. It doesn't seem like a good idea to break the poor lady's toe. Mrs. Capone picks up the handbag and gives it back to Piper.

"Oh, thank you! I'm so sorry. Terribly clumsy of me," Piper says. "As long as I have your attention, I was wondering . . ."

But it's too late. Mrs. Capone has her nose back in her letter.

Behind me I hear Rocky wind up another howl. Mrs. Capone hears him too. Her head turns to the sound. When she sees Rocky, her whole face seems to light up like somebody flicked a switch in her head.

"Mrs. Capone," Piper says, apparently forgetting she isn't supposed to know her name, "let me introduce you to baby Rocky."

Mrs. Capone ignores Piper. She's already on her way to Theresa, who is struggling with the howling infant while Jimmy hops on one foot, singing "Farmer in the Dell."

Mrs. Capone is standing right next to Theresa now. "O be-be-be," she coos to Rocky. Then she taps Theresa lightly on the sleeve. "Me?" she offers.

Theresa has been so busy with Rocky, she hasn't figured out this is Al's mom. She happily hands Rocky over to Mrs. Capone. Jimmy hesitates. He seems unable to decide what to do.

Mrs. Capone takes Rocky in her arms and rocks him gentle and wide like a large cradle. Almost immediately, as if by some spell, Rocky stops crying. Mrs. Capone keeps rocking, her smile broad and sweet.

"Mrs. Capone!" Piper won't give up. But Mrs. Capone ignores Piper and everyone else. She's busy singing a soft sweet lullaby in what I'm guessing is Italian. As far as she's concerned, there's no one else on the boat but that black-curly-haired baby. She sings to him all the way to Alcatraz.

When the boat docks, baby Rocky is asleep.

Mrs. Capone sighs. She hands the peacefully sleeping infant back to Theresa Mattaman. Then the light in her face goes dark, and she gathers herself together and walks slowly forward. Officer Johnson meets her and speaks with her for a moment, though Mrs. Capone's blank look makes me wonder if she understands any English at all. Then he leads her through the metal detector snitch box, which blares its sharp alarm bell.

"Ohhh," Theresa cries.

"For crying out loud." Jimmy whistles.

"The old lady's got a piece. She's going to break him out!" Piper cries, her mouth hanging open in complete surprise.

"Oh my God, Rocky! Are you all right?" Theresa holds him close.

"What were you thinking, giving him to her?" Jimmy hollers at Theresa.

Mrs. Capone says something. I can't understand the Italian words, but it seems like she's begging him not to do something. Officer Johnson's billy club is out. He points for her to follow. Officer Johnson and now Officer Trixle escort her to a small storage room under the dock. Other guards press close and

Officer Bomini up in the tower trains his Thompson on Mrs. Capone.

A minute later Officer Johnson comes out. "Jimmy! Your mom speaks Italian? Run get her! Fast!"

When Theresa hears this, she scoots up the hill with Rocky. She's just out of sight when Mrs. Mattaman comes down the stairs wearing shoes but no stockings. A hat but no sweater. She half runs down the stairs to the dock and disappears inside the storeroom.

We wait, hanging around as close as the three guards will let us. When Officer Johnson and Mrs. Capone finally come out, she's all messy-looking, like she dressed in a hurry. Her eyes are cast down. Mrs. Mattaman speaks Italian to her. Her voice is kind.

Mrs. Capone shakes her head. She won't look up. Instead of getting into the waiting truck to go up the hill to the cell house, Mrs. Capone gets back on the boat.

Later we learn that Mrs. Capone had been strip-searched to find her weapons. There were none. The metal stays on her old-fashioned corset set the snitch box off. And try as she might, Mrs. Mattaman could not convince the terrified Mrs. Capone that this humiliation was the last.

I can't get over this. I keep thinking about when Al Capone was a baby. I'll bet his mama sang him the same song she sang to Rocky. I'll bet she held his hand when they crossed the street, packed his lunch for school and sewed his name in his jacket—A. CAPONE so everyone would know it was his.

I'll bet she wishes she could do it all over again too . . . if only Al were little and she could.

23. SHE'S NOT CUTE

∎∎∎∎∎∎∎∎∎∎∎∎∎∎∎∎∎∎∎∎∎∎∎∎∎∎∎∎∎∎∎∎∎∎∎∎

Tuesday, April 2, 1935

In English class Miss Bimp pairs Scout and me together for a journalism project. And just like that we're friends again. We start talking about who we think will win the World Series this year. And the next thing I know, he's put a game together at lunch. He doesn't make a big deal out of it. Neither do I. If it weren't for the fact that my throwing arm is rusty and my timing stinks, I would be happy. But what do I expect? All I've done for the past two months is bowl.

Then on the way back to class Scout says, "I'll trade you my extra glove for one of those convict baseballs. You find one of 'em yet?"

"Not exactly."

"Piper said they just come sailing over the wall." He does a whistling imitation of a ball in flight. "She made it sound like everyone on Alcatraz has one."

"When you talk to Piper, anyway?" I ask as I stop to tie my shoes.

Scout waits for me. "Sometimes we talk in French class. How come you don't want to look for one?"

"I dunno." I heave my book bag over my shoulder and walk on.

"She said maybe she could get me one. Maybe," Scout says.

I stop and stare at him. "How come you're so friendly with her all of a sudden?"

He shrugs. "Kinda cute, don't you think?"

"No," I say.

Scout doesn't say anything. He throws his glove in the air and catches it.

"She's not cute." I glare at him.

"Fine, fine, she's not cute. What are you so ticked off about, anyway? I'm the one who's supposed to be sore, you know."

I kick at the grass. "I don't blame you for being burnt up."

"Piper said your sister is . . . different. She said nobody ever watches her but you." He looks quick at me and then away.

I shrug.

"Look, I'd just like to have one of those baseballs," he says.

"They look just like any other baseball."

"Oh, so you *do* have one."

"No, I don't." This comes out louder than I mean it to. "I've seen Jimmy's, that's all."

"Well, if they're laying around, I thought you could pick one up for me. You know, if we're friends . . ."

"Of course we're friends," I say. "Sure. I'll find you one." I smile at him.

In history class my teacher, Mr. Burger, begins discussing the Louisiana Purchase and I sit and stew.

It's not Scout I'm thinking about, though. It's Scout and Piper. Do they sit next to each other in French class? How come I haven't heard about this before? I knew they were friendly, but I didn't know they were that friendly. I think about this through history and all of math class. I think about it all the way home.

When my mother leaves, I unroll the sleeves of my shirt, button them at the cuffs, and I grab Natalie's jacket. There's poison oak on this island and I don't want us to get it.

"Okay, Nat, let's go." I open the door, all business today.

I head up the stairs, Nat scuffing along behind me, pulling at her sweater like her shirt sleeve is caught up inside.

"Hey, Nat," I say, doubling back so I'm walking next to her. As soon as I do, she stops dead in her tracks and refuses to move forward until I go first. Nat is a single-file girl. "What do you think of Mrs. Kelly?" I ask. I'm walking around to the windy west side of the island now, craning my neck back to hear what she says.

"9868," Natalie answers.

9868? What does that mean? Oh, yes, that's Mrs. Kelly's address. "Yes, exactly, 9868."

"No buttons, missy!" Natalie says. I look down at the water. There are almost waves today, like the bay is trying very hard to be the ocean.

"Right, I know. She won't let you play with your buttons." But there's something odd about the way Nat says no buttons.

"Naow bah-tins, mizzy." Natalie tries again, and this time I hear it. She's doing an imitation of the way Mrs. Kelly talks. Natalie has made a joke. It's the funniest thing I've ever heard.

For a second, I think I see Natalie smile too. Or maybe I've just imagined it. It's that quick.

I want to grab Natalie. Hold her here with me. Keep her from going down again. I just love talking to her this way. And then the thought occurs to me . . . is Mrs. Kelly helping?

"So, Nat," I say, like I would to a normal sister, "what would you think about two people who talk all the time in French class?"

"Two people talk," she says.

"Yeah, exactly."

She stops and looks at me. Right at me. Then it's almost as if she shrugs. Okay, so I'm probably wrong, but I like thinking this, even if it's not true.

"Okay, Nat," I say, eyeing the rec yard wall through the chain-link fence and straight up the hill from us. "We're looking for a baseball." I wait for the gulls to quiet down. "You know, like mine, right?"

"A line drive down the center . . ."

I smile. "That's right. We look for the baseball in the bushes here. Natalie look for baseball?" I say.

Natalie looks up in the sky as if it's going to fall from there.

"Well, not exactly. You look down here." I poke around in the bushes, showing her what I want her to do.

Natalie runs her tongue over her lip, as if this takes all the concentration she has.

"Okay, follow me." I shimmy up the steep hill sideways and begin picking through the thicket of bushes. I try to walk in a pattern. Natalie likes patterns, maybe she'll follow along. But it's difficult to keep to it because the bushes are thick. I look up at the yard wall again. My dad said the baseball diamond is in this corner. I scramble on through the underbrush.

Natalie isn't following. She's sitting down on the side of the hill with a pile of pebbles. She's setting them up, almost like an abacus. I wonder what she's doing. It seems complicated, but it looks like it's more fun than getting scratched by bushes, looking for a baseball. Sometimes Natalie is saner than I am.

I finish searching one patch, then look up at the chain-link fence that separates where I'm allowed to go from where I'm not. My eyes follow the chain link all the way up to where it hits the cement yard wall.

I can see the guard tower now, but I don't think the guard can see me. I look down at Natalie. She's totally absorbed in her stones.

I don't want Piper to find a ball for Scout. I don't know why, but I don't. I renew my search, looking inside every bush, kicking aside the leaves underneath. I'm right up against the chain-link fence now. The rec yard wall is solid cement—maybe sixteen feet high. But right where the chain link meets the cement wall, I see a gap.

The hillside has crumbled away, leaving a space between the fence and the mountain. Is this new? Did the mountain erode in all the rain? My heart beats loud in my throat.

I look down at Natalie. She hasn't moved a muscle. I won't be able to see her once I get up there. But I know better than to try to move her once she's all set up.

I'll just make it quick, that's all. A couple of seconds to look. One minute, that will be enough. A ball could be sitting right there out in the open, just waiting for me. I know this is a lousy idea. But it doesn't matter. A gap in the fence is a magnet. It just is.

24. LIKE A REGULAR SISTER

▪ ▪

Same day—Tuesday, April 2, 1935

It takes me longer than I thought it would to get to the gap. The hill is steep and slippery with rocks and shale, land sliding down as I go up. But the guard can't see me here. A chink in the hill blocks his view.

When I get to the hole in the fence, I wonder if I'll fit. The only way to tell if a ball is there is to look under the bushes, and I can't do that from over here. But what if I get stuck under the fence, what will I do?

I wish I could see Natalie. I should just go back and forget about this, but then I spot a little glimmer of grayish-whitish something resting on a rock. A baseball? I search for a stick to poke under the fence to see if I can roll the ball my way. It's not close enough. Only way to find out is to go under.

I sit down with a bump and stick my feet through. I scoot forward and get my knees under. This is taking too long. I have to check on Natalie. I lose my nerve and scoot back. But then I remember how hard it was getting up here. It'll take twice as long if I have to go back to see her and then climb the shale slide again. Didn't my mom say I should treat Natalie like a regular sister? I wouldn't go and check on a regular sister, that's for sure.

I stick my legs under again. Now I'm up to my waist. The

zigzag chain link at the bottom pokes into my belly, but I wiggle through. The only problem now is my big shoulders. "Football shoulders," my uncle Dean calls them. I wiggle wiggle wiggle, inch inch, turn my head and curl under.

Now I race for the ball, but I slow down as I get close. My throat gets tight. This is not a ball. It's just a piece of cardboard. I turn it over. The back says *Circle Janet T.* Janet Trixle. It's a project from the kindergarten class.

I'm so angry, I want to tear the circle up. But I don't. I shove it in my pocket. Then I think of Natalie. "Cut your losses," I hear my dad say. I'm going straight back to her. Only, I just have to peek one or two more places. It kills me to have risked all of this for nothing. Piper will get a ball for Scout and he'll think I didn't even try. Scout and Piper. Piper and Scout. But all I find is dirt, sticks, stones, leaves.

Now I feel like a real chump. I scoot myself back under, scratching my hand on the fence. At least I don't get stuck, I tell myself as the count bell rings. The little hairs along my spine stand up. I should never have left Natalie alone here. When it's really foggy, they don't let the cons work. Is it that foggy today?

I slip-slide down the hillside as fast as I can. And there she is. Her blonde-brown head bent over her rocks. She's sorting them. Of course she is. Everything is fine. I blow air out in a great big sigh.

I'm standing by Natalie now. She doesn't look up.

"Hey, Nat. Everything okay here? You just been playing your game, right?"

"105," she says.

"105?" I ask, trying to catch my breath as the foghorns

sound again. "Is that how many rocks you have? Wow, that's a lot." I hope she doesn't plan on lugging 105 rocks home. I look closer. She has thirty, maybe forty. Nowhere near 105 of them.

I look up at the birds. There are fifteen or so. Still, a big flock could have landed here while I was up there. She could have counted 105 birds. Sure. Easy.

"Lots of birds, huh? 105. Wow!" I say.

She looks up from her rocks. I see by the slight motion of her head that she's counting the birds down by the water.

"Bad Moose," she says. "Thirteen."

"Thirteen now, 105 before. They come and go, don't they, Natalie?"

"Thirteen." She's irritated now, like I'm being incredibly stupid. "Natalie count birds thirteen."

"All right, all right," I say. "Thirteen."

25. MY GAP

....

Wednesday, April 24, 1935

Every day at school now I play baseball with Scout at lunch. And though he hasn't said anything else about the convict baseballs, I know he's thinking about it. I know because Piper tells me. She asks me if I'm going to get Scout a ball. She asks more than once. Both times I pretend I don't hear, but Natalie and I hunt every day. I draw diagrams of the arcs a ball might take from inside the prison wall to the free space outside. Nat and I look for three days straight near the northeast point by the water tower. I feel like I work the place over with a pick and ax. But nothing.

It's not like Nat really helps me, but she doesn't get in my way either. She sits and counts rocks or sticks or sometimes birds. I always make sure to park her right in the center of where I want to look so I can keep an eye on her. We're getting along, Nat and I. It's peaceful to spend time with her out here. Sometimes I even tell her stuff that's bothering me. I don't know if she understands, but she's quiet like she hears.

The other place I always go is the gap. Last night I dreamt Scout found the gap. It's my gap. The thought of Scout worming his way through *my* hole in *my* fence and finding *my* ball makes me nuts.

This afternoon the teachers have a meeting, so we get out of school an hour early. I hope my mother doesn't know this, but when I get home, I see she does. She has an errand to run in the city. She's ready to leave just like always.

As soon as she's gone, I head straight for the gap, with Natalie toe-stubbing along behind me. She's wearing a green dress with puffed sleeves and some kind of pucker stitching across the top. It's a dress a ten-year-old should wear. Natalie looks silly in it. She's too old.

We cut through the parade grounds, where Annie, who had the day off from school, and Theresa are huddled over something. "Hey," Annie says. "Where've you been? Want to toss a ball around?"

"I can't now," I say.

"Where are you going?" Theresa glances up from the card she's working on. *Machine Gun Kelly,* it says.

"Oh, you know . . . looking for a convict ball," I say.

Annie's almost-white eyebrows raise. "I thought you didn't care about that. . . ."

"Well, I don't. Didn't. But now I do. Just, you know—kind of," I say.

"For Piper?" Annie asks, the corner of her mouth twitching like she's fighting a smile.

"For me," I shoot back at her.

"You'll never find one over there, but go ahead," Annie says.

I look hard at her. "Where will I find one?"

"Beats me. All I know is the balls don't go over very often," Annie says.

"How'd you get one?" I ask.

"My dad got it for me."

"Is that how Piper got hers?"

"I dunno," Annie says.

"Can I come?" Theresa asks.

"I thought you wanted to finish," Annie says.

Theresa looks at me, then Annie. She chews her bottom lip.

"You can go if you want," Annie tells her.

Theresa shakes her head. "We have to finish," she says.

"If you feel like playing later . . ." Annie nods to me.

"Sure," I say as Natalie and I head down the steps. Above us six or seven birds track her. I swear every bird on the island knows Natalie.

We stop near the greenhouse, below the southwest corner of the rec yard wall. We've got this down to a system, Natalie and I. In some ways she is very predictable, more like a clock than a human being. I set her up with a big pile of rocks and she's fine.

It's a warm, clear spring day. I feel happy, as if I'm on the verge of something wonderful. No matter what Annie says, I'm going to find a baseball today. I even start whistling "Take Me Out to the Ball Game."

When we get to the spot by the west end, I notice the terraces. They are full of new pink, yellow and bright purple garden flowers growing in neat rows. Across the water, I look to see how they're doing on the Golden Gate Bridge today. Progress is slow. It always looks the same. The Bay Bridge too, though I can't see it from here.

Natalie breaks her graham cracker sandwiches carefully along the dotted lines, eats half and throws the other half to the birds. Then she gets busy gathering her stones. She's very diligent about this, like it's her job. I start up the hill.

When I get to the gap in the fence, I kick more of the hill

away first before I try to fit through. Why didn't I think of this before?

Okay, I'm in. "Let's be smart, Moose," I tell myself. I'll begin at one corner and search every square inch until I get to the other. Slowly, carefully I look under each bush, marking my progress so I don't get confused about which bushes I've checked and which I haven't. "Take your time," I say out loud. "Keep your mind on business."

For a while everything goes okay. But then I start getting discouraged. No baseball. It's not fair. I'm doing everything right. I look again and again and again. Nothing, nothing, nothing.

Maybe there just aren't any more balls out here, I think for the hundredth time. Maybe this is all a big fat waste of time. I scoot back under the fence, too fast this time, and rip the back of my shirt.

Then I slide back down the shale to the halfway spot. A gull is pecking at the dirt, scouting for leftover graham cracker crumbs. Five piles of stones are neatly sorted by size. But Natalie . . . where is Natalie?

26. CONVICT BASEBALL

▪▪▪▪▪▪▪▪▪▪▪▪▪▪▪▪▪▪▪▪▪▪▪▪▪▪▪▪▪▪▪▪▪▪▪▪▪

Same day—Wednesday, April 24, 1935

"Natalie," my mouth tries to say, but my throat is closed up tight. No sound comes out. I run down, my arms flying helter-skelter, the shale sliding.

She has to be here. Maybe she's out scouting for more stones. That's it. I look down by the small rocky beach. A crab scuttles out from under a rock. Men on a nearby ferry are laughing; the sound is eerily loud though the boat is far away. She isn't there. Over by the red berry bushes. No. Back by the greenhouse. No. Which way do I go?

I stop and listen. A voice . . . sounds. Behind me.

I spin and run toward the voice. "Natalie?" I crash the thicket. And then I see her. Natalie sitting on a rock with someone. A man. He is wearing a denim shirt and denim pants. A con. Natalie is sitting with a con.

The scream is stuck in my throat, choking me. Don't look away. Don't blink. Do not blink.

The con is smiling. He's missing a front tooth. There are dark greased comb marks in his hair. I wonder about this. Inmates aren't allowed hair pomade. Suddenly this seems very important. Why is he wearing pomade on his hair? Maybe he isn't a con. Please, God, don't let him be a con.

I haven't even looked at Natalie. I'm afraid to take my eyes off the guy in the denim shirt. I think somehow I can protect her this way. But now I watch her too. She's smiling. Sometimes Nat looks concerned or sad, or raging mad. The best she ever looks is interested. But here is my sister, Natalie Flanagan, looking happy.

"Hey, Moose." The con's voice is scratchy and an octave too high, like a girl's almost. "You want this?" He reaches inside the coat draped over his leg. He has a gun. I can't breathe. He's going to shoot. But then I see. Information seeps into my brain. It isn't a gun.

It's a baseball.

Suddenly, my throat opens up. "Get a-way. . . . Get the heck away! Go! Go! THAT'S MY SISTER! GET AWAY FROM HER!" I scream as the four o'clock count whistle blows. The con jumps and Natalie's smile, like some kind of rare bird sighting, slips away.

"Take it easy, fella. I got your baseball, didn't I?" the con says. He nods at me and turns to Natalie. "Bye, sweetie." He closes Natalie's fingers around the baseball and fast walks away.

"DO NOT. DO NOT CALL HER SWEETIE," I shout. His pace is uneven, like one leg is shorter than the other. Then I see the number stamped on the back of his denim shirt: 105.

27. IDIOT

■ ■

Same day—Wednesday, April 24, 1935

"Nothing happened." I say this out loud to shut up the voice in my head. My teeth are chattering like I'm cold. They were just sitting there. There's no law against that. But I can't stop thinking what the warden told me the first week we came here. "Some of these convicts haven't seen a woman in ten or fifteen years. I think you're old enough to understand what that means. . . ." I was only gone two minutes, three minutes, maybe. No more. N-O M-O-R-E. N-O-T-H-I-N-G H-A-P-P-E-N-E-D. The words go round and round in my head like the wheels of a car rolling over the slats of a bridge.

But it was more than three minutes. Way more. I left right after the three o'clock count whistle, I returned before the next. I was probably gone forty-five minutes. NO. I left way after the three o'clock whistle. It was only ten minutes. NO MORE.

Calm down, I tell myself. Nothing happened. My mind flashes on the greasy-haired con holding my sister's hand, and a sick feeling comes over me. My mouth tastes like curdled milk.

I don't know what happened. I wasn't there.

I'm so upset, I hardly see where I'm going. Natalie is pulling back, trying to go slow. I tug her along. I don't care what she wants.

We're almost to the west stairs now and I'm not even sure how we got here. It's like I dreamed the distance.

How did he know my name? How did he know what I was looking for? He had that ball with him. He must have known before. 105, that was the number that didn't make sense. IDIOT. I AM AN IDIOT. Natalie must have said something the last time. THE LAST TIME WE WERE OVER HERE. COULD THAT BE? He must have left before I saw him then. Probably meant to today. But he brought the ball. Insurance, I guess. Figured he could buy me off.

I grip Natalie's arm so tight, it feels as if I'm holding bone. She tries to twist her arm away, but I'm not about to let go. Ever. She balks. Stops. Refuses to be half-dragged when we both know she follows just fine without this. But I won't give her even this much freedom. "What's the matter with you? Don't you know the first thing about *anything*?" I scream. "Come on! Can't you just walk with me for once?"

Almost there, almost there. I'm going to cry and I sure as heck don't want to do it out here. I pray Theresa isn't there waiting. I don't want to find her sitting outside our door. We turn the corner to our landing and my chest falls.

Someone is there. Piper. Oh, man, just what I need!

Piper's hat is tipped to the side. She's watching me out of the corners of her eyes.

"You were chewing out Natalie. You were yelling at her," Piper says.

"I wasn't."

"Yes, you were! I heard you. You never yell at her. What's going on?" she demands.

I keep my mouth shut and stare at the doorknob, wishing I could get Piper out of the way.

Piper looks at Natalie. Natalie is rubbing her chin on her shoulder, her chin on her shoulder, faster than normal, as if she's upset too. Have I done this or was it 105? She seemed happy with that greasy-haired con, so it was probably me.

"Sweet Jesus." Piper whistles one long note. "You found a ball. That's one of ours, isn't it?"

She holds her hand out to Natalie.

Natalie can be very possessive with her things. She would never give anyone a rock or a button. I think Piper will be in for a fight. But no. Natalie plops the ball in Piper's hand, easy as can be.

"Where did you find it?"

I don't look Piper in the face. I feel like I held my sister hostage for that stupid baseball. I won't touch it. It's dirty. The last thing in the world I want is to tell anyone how we got it. And Piper is ten times worse than just anyone. How could I have let this happen?

"105," Natalie says.

I say nothing. It feels like all the blood is draining out of my face. I'm light-headed. Please, Piper, be as stupid as I was.

Piper is frowning. She's trying to understand. Do not figure this out. *Do not figure this out.*

"105 what?" Piper asks. She pushes the brim of her hat back, as if to see better. She is staring intently at Natalie.

Natalie says nothing. Good Natalie.

"We gotta go inside." I touch the door. It feels good, that door. I can almost hear the sound it will make when it slams shut.

"Come on! 105 what? Is that how many places you looked? What?" Piper asks. She's standing firm between me and the door. Her hands are crossed in front of her and the frilly blouse she wore to school is tucked inside her overalls. Even as upset as I am right now, some part of me registers how cute she is.

"Because I haven't heard of a ball going over in months. I didn't think you'd find one," Piper says.

"Thanks a lot." I snort. "You could have told me that. You know I've been looking."

"I'm your baby-sitter now too?"

"Pocket," Natalie says, picking wildly at her shoulder.

"Pocket?" Piper asks me.

Usually I don't like when people talk to Natalie through me. I'm not a ventriloquist and Natalie isn't my dummy, but today I want her mute. "She doesn't mean anything by that," I lie.

"Yellow buttons," Natalie says, taking two buttons out of her pocket.

"Natalie's upset. We need to go inside." I try to edge Piper out of the way. But Piper isn't budging.

"Stop, Natalie. You have to tell me." Piper recrosses her arms in front of her chest. She's pulling rank. Only Natalie couldn't care less whose daughter Piper is.

"105," Natalie says.

"105 buttons?" Piper squints. She looks at Natalie, then me, then Natalie again. A big slow smile pours across her face. "Oh, sweet Jesus, you don't mean . . ."

I twist the knob and try to knee open our door.

"You got a con to give you a ball, didn't you? How did you do that? And who the heck is AZ 105? Somebody on the dock? I HAVE TO KNOW!"

I have the door open and I'm trying to pull Natalie inside while keeping Piper out.

"Was it a waiter at the Officers' Club? Was it?"

"Natalie, come on!"

"Wow, Moose, I never thought you'd do something like this!" She smiles big.

My insides boil up and I barely restrain myself from slugging her. I push Natalie inside our apartment, then I try to get past Piper.

"What did you give him for the ball?" Piper asks.

I've got my shoulders in and I'm trying to close the door now. If only I can get Piper's fingers out of there.

"C'mon. You must've given him something," Piper asks.

"Move your hand! And shut up," I cry.

"This is amazing!" Piper says, her eyes glowing. I've never seen her so excited. "Think maybe he could get autographs too, Moose? Because Al Capone's signature, that is worth a fortune! This is the beginning, Moose!"

"NO! THIS IS THE END!" I shut the door in her face.

28. TALL FOR HER AGE

▪▪▪

Same day—Wednesday, April 24, 1935

The thing to do is come clean. Talk to my mom. Talk to my dad. Tell them. They'll understand. It was an accident. Three minutes. Five at the most. My mom said to treat Nat like a regular sister. Well, I certainly would leave a regular sister for five minutes. My mom can't be mad. Together we'll work out the right thing to do so this will never happen again.

I can hear my mom's footsteps on the landing. She bursts in the door.

"Look, Moose!" She waves a newspaper in the air. She slaps it on the table. "See! Didn't I tell you what a wonderful program they have? It's world famous! Look, it says right here."

NEW HOPE FOR KIDS WITH MENTAL DEFICIENCIES, the headline reads. There is a picture of Mr. Purdy standing in front of the Esther P. Marinoff and a small close-up of a boy. *Tom, age 10, was mute when he came to the Esther B. Marinoff, but now he speaks in simple sentences and reads at a third-grade level,* the caption reads.

The article is filled with quotes from experts. *The program is quite extraordinary. It's modeled after a school in Switzerland run by the behaviorist Emil Binder.* I skim down to see what Mr. Purdy has to say. *"Entrance in the school is highly selective. We have a small number of spaces for kids who are truly ready for the kind of opportunities we offer. Children start at the Esther P. Marinoff when they are 7 to 12 years of age and typically graduate at 18,"* Mr. Purdy says.

How old does Mr. Purdy think Natalie is? Does he really believe she's ten?

My mom has taken off her green hat and her green coat and she has begun to make supper. Every minute or so she comes back to the table to read a part of the article again. It's as if the newsprint is warm and my mother's hands are very cold.

Natalie is on the living room floor, reading my math book like it's the newspaper.

"Mom, I need to talk to you," I say.

"Okay, honey." She smiles. "I can't wait to tell your dad about this! And do you know what else?" My mom claps her hands. "Mrs. Kelly says Natalie is really improving. She's going to write her a flying-color recommendation. That's what she said. Flying colors!" My mom hugs me. She's so happy, she would hug the saltshaker if it were only taller. "Your sister is going to be okay! She's going to be fine!"

"But, Mom," I say, "it says no kids are accepted after the age of twelve!"

My mother freezes. She's so still, it looks like she's stopped breathing. "Natalie is ten, Moose. You know that." Her voice has a catch in it.

"You can't be ten for five years in a row," I whisper.

"MOOSE!" my mother cries. Her eyes are like teeth tearing into me.

I remember that funny look Mr. Purdy had on his face when

he asked if Natalie was ten. All I see in my head is Natalie holding hands with a grown man. "I can't stand this anymore, Mom," I say.

"She's tall for her age. What's got into you?"

I look down at the article. "I need to talk to you."

"Fine, we'll talk tonight, your dad will be home any minute. Didn't I already say that?" She slams down a square pan. It makes a tinny sound against the counter.

Now I wish I hadn't said anything at all to my mom. I should have just talked to my dad about this.

When my father walks in the door, my mother rushes to meet him. "Cam, look!" She hands NEW HOPE FOR KIDS WITH MENTAL DEFICIENCIES to my father.

"This is a red-letter day," my father agrees. He takes my mom in his arms and does a little jig in the kitchen.

I can't stand to watch this. I head for my room.

"Hey, Moose," my father says later that night when Natalie is in bed. "Mom says you want to talk to us."

"Yeah," I say, my heart beating loud and guilty in my chest. I close my book, wishing they had forgotten.

"I don't think it's safe for Nat to follow me around," I say.

My mother stares at me like she can't believe what I've just said. "But, Moose ... she's doing so well. Carrie Kelly thinks we shouldn't change one thing, because being out with you kids and working one-on-one with her is the best possible—"

"Something happened." I feel nothing when I say this, like my mouth is talking all by itself.

They wait.

"What happened?" my dad asks. He touches my arm, gently.

My mind is scrambling. How can I tell them without really telling them? "I don't think it's safe for her on this island. She doesn't understand stuff. It's dangerous."

"What happened?" my father asks again.

"A con noticed her today," I say. My words feel like they are weighted down with stones.

My father sighs and sticks a toothpick in his mouth. "Well, I can't say I'm surprised, Moose, but I understand how upsetting that would be."

My mother glares at him. "A con whistled at her. Is that it? She's a pretty little girl, your sister. I wish I had a penny for every time some guy whistled at me. Let's not lose sight of what's important here."

"Honey, wait." My father takes her arm again.

"No, *you* wait. Natalie is getting better. Do you know what she said yesterday? She said, 'You made me sad.' Do you think I like making her sad? I don't. But she's never said anything like that before. 'What is 55,031 times 59,032.' 'Does May 16 fall on a Wednesday in 1914?' This she's said. But never *you*—not *Mommy*—*you*, a pronoun. I've been trying to get Natalie to use pronouns her whole life. And feelings . . . she said something she felt. Natalie is communicating with us . . . this is so important! There's no way she'll be turned down at the Esther P. Marinoff now—"

"It's dangerous, Mom."

"Dangerous? Nothing on this island is half as dangerous as having her locked in her own world. Not one half, not one fourth, not one tenth as dangerous as that. So, I am not, do you two hear me, NOT GOING TO CHANGE ONE SINGLE THING ABOUT NATALIE'S DAY! Things are going too well. And, Moose, I won't have you sulking inside with her all afternoon!"

This smarts. I can't believe she said this. "I've been taking her with me *everywhere*! I haven't been sulking!"

"No, of course not." My father's hand cups my neck. "You've been a major reason why Natalie is doing so well, and your mother and I understand that."

My mother glares at my father. She's really angry now, but I am too. No matter how hard I work, it's never enough. She walks out of the room, then back in. "The entrance interviews for the Esther P. Marinoff are only four weeks away. We're so close. I don't want anything to go wrong." Her voice cracks.

"Calm down, honey. Nothing's going to go wrong," my father says. "It's not.

"Moose"—he turns to me—"thanks for bringing this to our attention. But I need to talk to your mom for a minute alone."

29. CONVICT CHOIR BOY

. . . .

Wednesday, May 1, 1935

The next week I do my best to stay away from Piper. But the more I steer clear, the more she seems to want to be around me. "She's planning something. Watch yourself," Annie tells me on Monday.

On Wednesday I find out Piper has given Scout 105's baseball, and then she's stopped talking to Scout. I guess she doesn't need him anymore. And Scout doesn't seem to care, which surprises me even more. "You can have her, Moose," he tells me while we're warming up for our lunch game. "She's more trouble than she's worth."

"Oh, great," I say. "Gee, thanks."

"I think she's googly-eyed for you, anyway," he says.

"No, she isn't," I tell him.

Scout nods his head. "You like her too, and you know it."

"I don't know what you're talking about," I tell him. It isn't possible to like someone I dislike as much as Piper. It didn't used to be possible, anyway.

"So, Moose, we're friends, right?" Piper corners me as I come out of the bathroom right after the last bell at school.

"Whatever you say, Piper." I pick up my books and head out the door into the bright sunshine.

"And friends help each other, right?"

I don't like the sound of this.

"I need your help." She touches my hand.

I close my eyes, blow air out of my mouth and walk faster.

She keeps pace with me. "I want your help with 105. You have an in now. Natalie does, anyway."

"You are unbelievable." I spit the words out at her.

"Moose, wait! Come on!"

"I don't want to talk to you, Piper. I just don't." I keep walking fast, my head down.

"This is going to help you too. Because otherwise you'll always wonder. You'll never know what happened between Natalie and 105."

"I know what happened. I was there," I lie.

"No, you weren't," she says.

"Go cram your head in the crapper, Piper," I yell in her face, and cross the street to get away from her. How does she know everything?

"Look," she wheedles, keeping pace with me. "You've been driving yourself nuts with this, haven't you, Moose? But we can fix that. We'll let Natalie go to meet 105 and then we'll spy on them. Then you'll know. And if 105 tries anything, you can pound him, right, Moose? Won't that feel good?"

"As far as I'm concerned, 105 does not exist."

"We came so close to getting into the cell house with Mrs. Capone," Piper says.

"No, we didn't," I say.

"What if they'd used Jimmy or Theresa to translate instead of Mrs. Mattaman? And then they'd need to take them up to the cell house, because cons can't talk to visitors in a foreign language."

"What if, what if, what if. None of that even came close to happening."

"Didn't you learn anything? Just be there. Just be close and it will happen. You can't catch a ball unless you're in the ballpark! Take 105 for example," she tries again.

"I don't know what you're talking about," I shout, stopping in the middle of the sidewalk.

"Natalie certainly does. That's all she talks about is 105."

I glare at her. "How would you know?"

"I heard her one day when she was with your mom. Your mom had no idea what she was talking about, but I knew," Piper says.

My neck gets stiff. I can hardly move it. "She loves numbers is all. That's always what she talks about." I start walking again.

"Oh, yeah, right. Look, what's the harm of just talking to the guy, 105?"

"No harm. Go ahead. You don't need me and you don't need Natalie."

"Ahhhh." She makes a disgusted noise and cuts in front of me.

"Well, you don't." I sidestep her.

She cuts me off again. There's an odd expression on her face, both eyes looking left, not at anything in particular.

"What?" I ask.

She scratches her back. "Well . . ." She sighs.

"Well what?"

"I tried to talk to 105, but he wouldn't talk to me."

"No kidding. You know, you really charmed Mrs. Capone too. I mean, dropping your purse on her toe. What a nice touch!"

"Shut up."

"What did the guy do, anyway? Homicide? Kidnapping?" I can't stop myself from asking this.

"I dunno, but he's only got one more year. Not even that, half a year, I think. That's why he has so much freedom. They figure he wouldn't run with six months to go. It wouldn't be worth it to jeopardize that. You think they'd let just any old convict wander around the place *gardening?* Plus, the guy—they call him Onion because the way his hair is greased down makes his head look like an onion—he's put together a whole slew of good time. He's like some kind of Boy Scout choir boy."

"Choir boy?" I ask.

"Kind of like you . . . convict choir boy from the root vegetable family." She smiles.

"How'd you find out?"

"I looked in my dad's files. Couldn't find what he was in for, but I found out he was on gardening detail. I went to the gardens. There he was. Surely, if *Nat* could find him, I could too."

"Nat's not stupid!" I shout.

"Did I say she was?"

"Say it! Say she's not stupid."

"She's not stupid." Piper shrugs and we start walking again.

I know I shouldn't talk to her anymore, but I can't help it. I have to know. "That true about him being a good guy . . . ?"

"Yep," Piper says. She looks me square when she says this.

I think about what a liar Piper is. Even so, what she says makes sense. Why would they let an escape risk have the run of the place? "If he won't talk to you, what makes you think he'll talk to Natalie?" I ask.

"Because he did already, idiot!"

"Jeez, Piper, why do you go sticking your nose in this?"

"What are you all bent out of shape about?" Piper asks, shifting her books to the other arm. "She's not pregnant, right?"

"Piper! For crying out loud!"

"You do know about the birds and the bees, don't you?"

"Shut up, Piper! Just shut up!"

"Did you ask her at least?"

"Look, this is off limits." I make a flattening gesture with my hands. "I just have to keep her safe until the Esther P. Marinoff interview."

"And then what?"

"And then she'll get in and get better and we'll all live happily ever after."

"What if she doesn't get in, though? I mean, she didn't before, right? What makes you think she will this time?"

This is the question my whole family has been avoiding. Just hearing Piper ask it out loud makes me feel disloyal.

"She will," I say. My voice comes out in a funny jerk.

Piper raises her eyebrows and studies me. "There's a chapel in the basement of the cell house. If she doesn't get in, then maybe she and 105 can get married. He's getting out soon."

"Piper, SHUT UP," I shout.

"Get mad all you want, but it seems perfectly reasonable to me. They could have babies."

"SHUT UP!" I feel a blinding urge to grab hold of Piper's throat.

"If she gets in, how long till she starts there? Can you at least tell me that?" Piper asks.

"I dunno for sure."

"So we better get going!" she says.

"PIPER, FORGET IT!"

"Wouldn't you like to know what happened?" Her eyes are burrowing inside me now.

"It's not safe, Piper."

"Why not? You're going to be right there. *We're* going to be right there."

"What is it to you, for chrissakes?" I glare at her.

"I want to meet Al Capone."

"This is just some guy. Some criminal choir boy Onion guy. It isn't Al Capone."

"Yeah, but it's a start. Who knows where it will lead."

I stare at Piper. Those squinty eyes. That cute little movie star mouth. That long straight hair. Then I get it. It isn't just about Al Capone. "You like to play with fire. You love being around all of this criminal stuff, don't you?"

"And you don't?"

I stare out at the water, busy with ferries and fishing boats. "Not half as much as you do," I say.

30. EYE

■ ■

Tuesday, May 7, and Wednesday, May 8, 1935

All I think about is telling my mom about 105. She'll say ugly things, but then it will be done. I'll never be given this kind of responsibility again. I'll go back to being a kid—the way I was before moving to this stupid turd-covered rock. Natalie will be safe and we can all move somewhere else. I would do this in a flash if it weren't for my father.

I can't stand to disappoint him again.

I try to forget all of this—try to stop the churning in my mind—but as soon as I do, Natalie mutters "105" and I'm back into it again. She's always had a "number of the week," as my father calls it. It's usually the number of buttons in her collection or shoes in my mother's closet or spools of thread in the drawer. Ever since the day I lost her, the number has been 105.

"105!" she says almost every day now, her hand on the door-knob and the hard force of her whole self headed out. But somehow I keep her inside. I let her play with her buttons and feed her four pieces of lemon cake while she sits by the door.

On Tuesday when my mother comes home, she seems to know we've stayed inside again. Of course, I've managed to separate Natalie from her buttons before my mom walks up the stairs from the dock. Even so, my mother knows. And when Natalie refuses to eat one bite of supper, so stuffed is she with lemon cake, my father knows too.

I hover around my father. When he says he has to help the warden with a project after supper, I offer to go with him—beg him, actually. I don't want to be left alone with my mom. But he says he can't take me. There's a problem in the cell house kitchen, where I'm not allowed to go.

"Moose," my mom says as soon as my father is gone.

"I have a lot of homework," I say.

My mother nods.

I can't bear this. It's in my head, the sentences I plan to tell her. The truth. I let my sister hold hands with a convict. They were alone together. Twice? Three times? I don't even know how many. I was over there looking six, seven times.

I wish I could make my mother understand how much more complicated this is than she thinks. But the only way to do this is tell her what happened, which I can't seem to do.

My mother doesn't yell about us staying inside. Not one critical word comes out of her mouth. She doesn't have to say anything. The air itself carries her blame. I feel it when I breathe.

We both keep our space, never passing close to one another, like magnets set to repel.

The next day, when the door closes behind my mother, Natalie says what she'd said all day long the day before. "105."

"No, Natalie. Not today. Today we're doing buttons," I say.

But the buttons aren't in her bureau drawer. They aren't on top of the icebox or in the cupboard by the stove. They aren't in my mom's closet or the bread box either. I turn the place upside down, searching every drawer twice. But I know I won't find them, because they aren't there. My mother has taken them with her. I didn't see her do this, but I know she has.

The only thing I can do is keep Natalie inside. I look for cake. One slim piece of lemon is all I find. Half a piece, really.

Natalie looks up at me. She has watched my feet as I've looked for her buttons. I can't tell if she knows exactly what's going on, but she knows something.

"Fine," I say, pulling open a drawer for the third time now. "Fine. We'll . . ." I let the sentence drift off, then I march to my room and get my math books and stack them by the door. We'll read math books all afternoon. I'll stand in front of the door. I won't let her pass. I'm stronger. I have forty, maybe fifty pounds on her.

Natalie is rocking wildly, like a little boat in a ship's wake.

"105," she says.

"No," I say.

"Buttons," she says.

"Numbers," I say, cracking open a book and offering it to her. "Look, Natalie, you can read about numbers."

"Buttons 105!" She's rocking crazy hard.

Why not just let her throw a fit? Why try so hard?

"OUTSIDE, buttons. 105." She's spinning now.

I try to ignore her. I open my book, but I read the same sentence over and over. The meaning won't go into my head. "Stop it, Natalie!" I yell.

But she's losing herself. The scream has started. It begins low, like a piece of machinery that needs time to warm up.

"Stop it, Natalie!" I holler loud in her face. "Stop being like this! Don't you see what you're doing? You're not a little kid, stop acting like one!"

She throws herself on the floor. She kicks the coffee table.

"Do you have any idea what you're doing to us? To Mom and Dad? You're making them old. They worry about you all the time. At least you can try. At least you can do that. Sometimes I think you don't even try and I hate you for it, Natalie. We try so hard and you don't. I hate you, Natalie! I do!"

A vase hits the rug. It thumps hard, but doesn't break.

She's near the windows now, twisting, banging feet, hands flailing on the floor. The more I yell, the more she screams, like we're trying to top each other. My shouts are full of words, hers are only sound. Animal sounds. Piercing and terrified.

There's banging outside. I see through the window Mrs. Trixle's brand-new red hair and short round Mrs. Caconi trying to see what's happening. I'm surprised she made it up the stairs so fast. Someone else is banging too.

"Moose! It's me, Theresa! Let me in!"

"Open up, Moose. What's going on in there?" Bea Trixle calls.

"I can help! You need me!" Theresa again.

"Theresa! Go back inside!" Bea Trixle cries.

"Stop it! Stop it!" I have my hands on Nat's arms. I want to shake her, shake her hard. My arms tremble with the effort not to.

Natalie screams louder. I look into those trapped eyes. Wherever she is, she can't get out, which only makes her scream louder. And suddenly I'm not angry anymore.

"Open the door, Moose!"

"We're okay!" I call, though I know how ridiculous this sounds.

"Please, Nat, don't do this." I run to the kitchen. "How about some lemon cake?" I plead. But she's well beyond lemon cake. She takes the cake, mashes it in her hand and throws the plate against the wall, busting it into a billion pieces. Her whole body is moving in all directions, as if each limb has its own plan.

All of a sudden I remember what my mother used to do. I pick Natalie up, screaming and fighting, her skull bashing against my chin, and set her as gently as I can on her back on one corner of the rug. She's moving so wildly, she kicks me in the shin, her hand boxes my ear.

It's hard to keep her in one place, but I grab hold of her waist and pin her down at one corner. I hold her and the corner of the rug and roll, tightly, gently, using my knees to keep her in. When the rug is all the way around her, I wait. And slowly the fight begins to leak out of her. With the tightness surrounding her, she feels safe, secure somehow.

She lays shaking, grateful and forlorn in the stained red carpet. I breathe in a dust-rug-sweat smell.

Mrs. Caconi and Mrs. Trixle are still banging on the door. They have gotten Mrs. Mattaman now. She's tall enough to see what's happening inside. She's holding baby Rocky.

I ignore them and talk to Natalie in a sweet calm voice, as if she were a baby too.

"Natalie, how can I help you?"

Natalie is quiet. Breathing hard. She's calm now except for her eyes, which seem to be moving back and forth in her head, as if they are still searching for a way out.

"You're okay now, Natalie." I stroke her tangled hair, my hand brushing against her hot wet forehead.

"Moose, Natalie outside," she says.

"Oh, Natalie." I shake my head.

"Eye," Natalie says.

"What? Something in your eye?" Her eyes have slowed down. I look to see if something is in them. I can't see anything.

"Eye."

"Yes, I know you were upset. That's why your eyes are moving around that way," I say.

"Eye," she says. She's calm now. I unroll the rug. She sits up. Both hands on her chest, petting it as if it has a full coat of fur. "Eye," she says again.

"That's not your eye, Natalie," I say. "That's your chest."

"Eye outside," Natalie says.

"You want to look outside?" I check to see if Bea Trixle and Mrs. Caconi and Mrs. Mattaman are still there. They're gone. Maybe they realized we were okay and went away. Or maybe they've gone to get a crowbar or my father. I look back at Natalie. Her face is scrunched up. It's crushed, as if she wants me to understand and I won't.

"Eye outside," she says loud, like I'm deaf.

I say nothing. I don't know what she wants.

Her face seems to close in with the effort. "Eye want to go outside," she says finally.

We're working on pronouns. My mom said this. Pronouns. Natalie, who never called herself anything but Natalie my whole life, just called herself "I."

"Oh," I say. "I want to go outside?" My voice breaks.

"I want to go outside," she says, the look of relief on her face as big as thirty states.

I open the door then. I do. How could I not?

31. MY DAD

■ ■

Same day—Wednesday, May 8, 1935

We go to the parade grounds. Natalie gets on the swings. There's a mom there with her four-year-old son. She pushes him. I push Natalie. She's too big and too old for this. Her hips are too large for the seat. I ignore this. I ignore them. She can pump herself, but I know she prefers to have me push. After a few minutes I notice her head is tipping to the side. I run around to the front, just in time to catch her as she falls forward. She's sound asleep. Tantrums exhaust her. I can sure see why. They exhaust me too.

I carry her home as best I can. She seems so solid. So big. A real grown-up person in my arms. I stop often, leaning her weight on a cement wall, the edge of a building, the banister.

I'm almost to the back stairwell when my dad finds us.

He doesn't ask what happened. He simply takes Natalie from me and I follow him to our apartment. We walk through the wild mess of our living room. Rug pulled out from the coffee table, vases upended in a puddle of water, broken plate slivers and lemon cake scattered everywhere. My foot crunches the china pieces as I follow my father to Natalie's room. He places her gently on her bed and covers her with her favorite purple blanket.

Then he goes to the icebox and opens a beer. He looks over at me, seems to think a minute, opens another and pours a full glass for himself and half a glass for me. My father rarely drinks and never with me. I had a few sips once at Pete's house, but I didn't like it much. That doesn't matter. What matters is he seems to understand.

In the living room, he sets his beer down, picks up the vase and puts it back where it belongs. I set my beer by his and get the broom. The room is silent except for the clock ticking on the mantel, the sound of sweeping and the clink of china pieces as my father drops them in the metal trash tin.

"Dad," I ask. "How come you always do what Mom tells you?"

My dad makes a funny sound, a kind of laugh through his nose. He says nothing and then, a full minute later, "I don't always."

"Most of the time."

My father swallows, considers this. "Yeah, most of the time I guess I do."

"How come?" I ask, sweeping a glass piece off the rug to the floor and up the incline to the dustpan.

My father takes a sip of his beer. "Things matter more to your mother than they do to me."

"What things?"

"Everything . . ."

"Everything?" I ask. I'm watching him now. Searching his golden brown eyes.

"Everything . . . except you." My father bites his lip. The tears well up. He turns away and busies himself tugging the rug back in place.

I strain my eyelids open and try to breathe the tears back in my head. I look down, then take a breath. "Dad?" I ask.

I'm going to tell him what happened now. I am.

"Yeah," he says.

"Did I cause Natalie to be the way she is?" The question seems to come from somewhere deep inside of me.

"Moose?" My father freezes, his eyes riveted on me.

"Something I did? You said she got worse when she was three. That's when I was born. Was it me?" I concentrate on the rug.

"Moose." My dad grabs my shoulders and he looks straight into my eyes. "I don't know," he says, taking a teary breath, "what caused Natalie to be sick. I don't think anyone knows that. But I do know this." He bites his lip, his voice so full of feeling, he's having trouble speaking. "Absolutely . . . absolutely for sure it had nothing, nothing at all to do with you."

32. THE BUTTON BOX

When my mother comes in, Natalie's button box clattering against the sides of her purse, she sees me with the beer. Her eyes register the shock.

"What happened? Where's Natalie?" she asks, her voice sharp and tight in her throat.

"Natalie's fine. She's asleep in her room," my father says. "But I need to talk to you."

"Me?" my mom asks, her voice high and childlike.

"Yes," my father says.

My mother's eyes dart to me and then back to my dad.

"Just you and I," my father says, cocking his head toward the bedroom. "I don't want to talk here."

My mother nods. She follows my father into the bedroom. At first it's quiet in there. Hushed voices muffled by the closed door. Then the voices get louder and more angry. My mother cries. My father is angry and firm. I hear my name. I walk closer to the door.

"Look," my mother says, "I'm not taking any chances with this. Mrs. Kelly says—"

"I know what Mrs. Kelly says. I'm talking about Moose now and what he thinks. He's good with Natalie. They've worked out a relationship. We have to respect that and trust him."

"Well, yes, but—"

"You have to let him care about her his way."

And then something I can't hear.

"I got one child who has everything," my mom says, "big, strapping, healthy, smart . . . makes people laugh. Got kids coming over looking for him night and day, just like at home. Little ones, big ones and the girls—they all like Moose. But Natalie, Natalie doesn't have the whole world looking out for her. She needs me."

"Moose needs you too."

"Fiddlesticks, Cam."

"You don't think he does?"

She sighs. "I suppose he does."

"You two never try to understand each other," my father says. "Little things become big things with you and Moose that quick." He snaps his fingers. "Couldn't you have just talked to him about the button box?"

My mom is quiet for a minute. When she begins talking again, her voice is too low for me to hear. Now both of them are speaking softly. They aren't mad anymore. I think about what my dad said. I think so hard, it makes my head ache.

In Natalie's room, she's still sleeping, but I feel better sitting in here with her. She's so peaceful when she sleeps. So normal. This is the sister I might have had. I see now the person we missed.

"Natalie," I whisper. "This is your chance." I smooth out her tangled hair. "You have to get into the Esther P. Marinoff this time, okay? Mom can't handle it if you don't."

PART THREE

33. THE SUN AND THE MOON

▪▪

Monday, May 27, 1935

As the day of Nat's interview approaches, my mother behaves as if her nerves have rotted and fallen apart like old rubber bands. She can't seem to sit still. Can't stop moving. Can't keep her eyes off Natalie.

The day before Natalie's interview is her birthday. We have countless discussions about this. Should we celebrate it? Will the celebration throw Natalie off her schedule, or will skipping Natalie's birthday upset her more? What kind of food should Natalie eat this week? What should she wear? Should she have more or less button time? More or less time with Mrs. Kelly? More or less math time? More or less time with me? No detail is too small to be considered.

And always we end right where we start. We'll keep Natalie's schedule the same this week and have a small birthday celebration just like we always do. But every night my mother seems to have to decide this all over again.

When Natalie's birthday finally arrives, my mother tries with all her considerable energy to make things appear normal.

"Remember, tomorrow is the interview," she tells me in a low voice.

"Mom." I roll my eyes. "How could I possibly forget that?"

She sighs. "You're right. I'm sorry." She pats my shoulder. "Just keep her quiet today. There's extra lemon cake, and of course, her buttons. If she wants to play buttons all day long, it's perfectly fine with me. Just make sure she doesn't have one of her fits. She'll be a wreck tomorrow if she does. It takes her a week to get over one of those."

"I know, Mom! I know."

"And you have my number at the Liebs'?" My mom wiggles her hands into her gloves.

"Yes, Mom."

"Maybe I should stay home." She tugs her glove off.

I hold my breath. I want my mom to stay home in the worst way. What if something goes wrong? "Would you?" I ask.

She shakes her head. "You're better with Natalie than I am." Her voice cracks. She doesn't look at me. She dabs at her eyes, her gloves back on now.

"I am?"

She nods, staring at the clasp of her purse. "I'll be home early. Let's just pretend this is a normal day." Her voice is strained. She leaves without saying good-bye to Natalie or to me.

Natalie is busy in her room. She's drawing pictures of the moon in all its phases. For the past few weeks Natalie has been obsessed with the moon. This is strange for her. She's always been fascinated by the sun, but she doesn't like to do anything but watch it rise. She has never wanted to draw pictures of the sun, the moon or anything else for that matter.

For once I get my book out without feeling bad about it. Natalie is content. I crack open *David Copperfield* and begin to read Chapter One, "I Am Born."

The next thing I know, I hear pounding on the door. Natalie

stops what she's doing. She doesn't look away from her page, but she doesn't move either, as if the pounding has frozen her solid.

I think about not answering the door. There's no one I want to see. Not today. Other people could upset Natalie. The pounding doesn't stop. Natalie doesn't move except to dig her chin into her collarbone.

Now it's quiet. No more knocking. The only sound is the wind blowing a door shut outside. Natalie seems to relax back into her work. But just as her pencil makes contact with the page, *knock, thud, knock.* Natalie's chin hits her collarbone and digs hard again.

If this keeps up, it'll make her crazy. I open the door.

It's Piper, her hat in her hand. An odd attitude for her.

"Go away," I tell her.

"Gee, thanks," she says.

"No offense, but I'm trying to keep Natalie quiet today. The interview is tomorrow."

"That's fine. I wanted to come in, not go out," Piper says.

"No, you need to stay out," I explain.

"Me? *I'm* not going to upset Natalie. She likes me," Piper says.

"I'm sorry," I say, my hand on the door.

Piper scoffs. "Can I at least say happy birthday?" She looks so earnest, so sincere, smiling her sweet smile. She's even prettier without her hat.

"How did you know it was her birthday?"

"Theresa told me."

I don't agree to let her in, but I must be easing my grip of the door, because the next thing I know Piper is standing inside our living room and the door is closed behind her.

"Happy birthday, Natalie." Piper squats down to where Natalie is resting on her elbows.

"Birthday Natalie," Natalie repeats. I feel a stab of pain when I hear this. Natalie has come a long way. I can tell because this sounds like the old Natalie. She isn't parroting like this hardly at all anymore.

"Nice moons you got there." Piper stands up again. "Okay," she says. "That's all I wanted to do."

I feel my eyebrows creep up my face.

"*See,* and you didn't trust me," Piper says as she brushes past me out the door.

I watch her walk away. It feels like a vacuum has sucked the air out of our apartment. Piper is taking the air with her when she goes. And suddenly I want her to stay.

I shut the door quick before I call her back.

Natalie is busy with her moons for another half hour. And I'm happily eating folded-over bread and butter sandwiches on the couch, my book in my lap, my legs across the arm of the chair. I look at Natalie. She's fine. I look down at the book again, and then I hear paper ripping. Natalie is tearing up the moons she's made one by one, her chin jerking wildly down to her collarbone and up. Down and up. Her eyes are beginning to storm over. Little torn pieces of paper float through the air, scattering everywhere.

UH-OH! I slap my book closed and jump up. I shouldn't have let her do the moons. It was too new. Too unfamiliar.

"Natalie," I say. "Forget those stupid old moons! Let's have some lemon cake. Lemon cake, Natalie!" For a second I have her. We'll sit down, we'll eat, it will all be fine. But then the forces inside her seem to collide. I can almost see the battle in her eyes. All at once, the storm seems to win. Her eyes are leaving.

"NATALIE! OUTSIDE!" I scream. I jump in front of her, rushing to unlock the door.

She follows me. She's trying. Trying to fight it.

Outside Nat seems calmer. She walks hunched over. She still seems wild, like the fight is raging inside her, but the walking is helping. Giving her someplace to go.

"Where do you want to go, Natalie?" I ask.

Nat says nothing.

"Okay," I tell her. "We'll just walk."

I shiver. I wish I'd remembered our jackets, but I'm afraid to stop her now. She looks too vulnerable. Teetering on the edge.

But she's following me. We'll walk until my mom gets home.

Out on the parade grounds we circle the cement once. Twice. If she wants to walk in circles all afternoon, that's okay with me. Then abruptly on the third rotation Natalie breaks off and heads to the west stairs. I run to catch up to her and get in front. But she isn't following now, she's going her own way, and then suddenly Piper is there. I can't believe it. It's like she has a magnet in her head that draws her to trouble.

"What's the matter?" she asks.

"Just out for a walk," I mutter.

Piper gives me a funny look, then falls in line behind me. Natalie is walking fast. I skip in front of her and begin a slow U-turn. Natalie doesn't follow me.

I grab her hand, but the angry way she shakes me off scares me. I don't dare do it again. She's walking down the west stairs now. "Natalie, look, rocks! Let's count them," I say, jumping in front of her again. But she shoves past me.

"It's okay, let her go," Piper says from behind me.

"Shut up, Piper!" I spit back at her.

"She wants to say good-bye," Piper says.

"Shut up, I said!"

Natalie walks on.

"Natalie, we don't need to go there anymore. We've already found a ball!" I say.

Natalie ignores me. Her head is down and she's walking fast, as if she's late for something.

It's late. He won't come. We're okay. The words repeat in my head as if the sound will make it so. My pulse is beating in my ears. I feel Piper's arm on my arm.

"Let her go," Piper says.

My feet slow down like they are suddenly too heavy to lift. I let Natalie get a few steps ahead.

I can't do this anymore. I can't make it right. I don't even know what right is.

I watch Natalie. I don't let her out of my sight, but I'm higher on the hill, climbing a parallel course, and Piper is behind me.

I breathe fast, short, shallow breaths. Nothing to worry about. See, see, he's not here.

And then he is. The black greased hair. The short bulbed nose. The deep pockmarked skin. The uneven walk. I could take him. I know I could.

"Natalie!" he says, pleasure and warmth in his voice.

"105, 105, 105," she says.

"How've you been, sweetie?" He smiles at her.

I stand up, ready to crash down through the brush. How dare he! I feel a grip on my arm. Piper pulls me back down.

"I didn't think I'd get to see you again before you shipped out," 105 says.

"How does he know?" I ask Piper.

"About her?" Piper snorts. "The cons know everything about us."

Onion's small, quick, greasy hand takes hers.

"Natalie hates holding hands," I whisper. The tears sting my eyes.

I stand up again, about to shout something, but nothing comes out.

"It's okay," Piper says. I stand still, quiet, shaking.

Natalie is holding hands with a man convicted of some awful crime. It's so strange, so awful and so . . . normal. Natalie doesn't look weird. She's my older sister. A sixteen-year-old girl holding hands with a man not much older than she is.

This is terrible.

This is good.

34. HAPPY BIRTHDAY

▪▪

Same day—Monday, May 27, 1935

We stay outside for the longest time. Counting and cataloging rocks and shells. Piper and I are Nat's helpers, doing exactly what she tells us to do. I've never known Piper to take orders from anybody before, but she is now. We are a team and Nat is in charge.

When we do finally get home, it's almost dark and my mother is there. She's in the kitchen frosting a cake. She has made a sign that says HAPPY BIRTHDAY, NATALIE and cut, curled and painted long strips of newspaper to make confetti streamers, exactly like the ones my mom made last year.

"How's my birthday girl?" my mom asks Natalie.

Natalie says nothing. She threads one newspaper streamer through her fingers.

"Piper," my mom says. "Maybe you'd like to come to Natalie's birthday party!"

Piper smiles her charm-school smile. "I'd love to, Mrs. Flanagan," she says.

My heart dips low in my chest. I don't want to have Piper here for Natalie's party. We never invite anyone else. I'm surprised my mom asked her.

I look at the cake my mother is frosting, the number "10" on the top, just like every other year.

"Seven o'clock tonight. Right after supper," my mother says.

"Shall I invite some of the other kids?" Piper asks.

"Oh, no. Let's keep it small, shall we?" my mom says. Her eyes avoid mine. The smile on her face is the one she uses when parents of an obnoxious piano student ask how he is doing.

I go in my room and don't come out until supper, which I wolf down without saying a word and then return to my room. I plan on staying here until the last possible moment, which comes way too soon for me.

"Hey, Moose! We're having a party out here!" Piper bangs on my bedroom door. She has a present wrapped in funny papers in one hand and a juice jar filled with lemonade in the other.

"Moose!" My dad comes in to where I'm sitting on my bed. "Did someone give you grumpy pills today?" He puts my head in an arm lock and gives my scalp a good knock.

"Quit it, Dad!" I say, but I can feel a smile creep on my face.

"Grumpy with a capital G," my father says. He winks at Piper, then whispers to me, "What's the matter? Isn't one girlfriend good enough?"

"I'm here as Natalie's friend. This has nothing to do with Moose," Piper announces as she pushes the sleeves of her sweater up past her elbows.

"Yes, well, I can see why," my father says. "Go get yourself a hat and act like you're at a party, Moose. You're getting a bad reputation with the girls!"

Natalie looks up from the handful of streamers in her lap. "Theresa," she says.

My father laughs. "Yes, you're right, honey. That's your brother's other girlfriend, isn't it?"

I go into the kitchen to get a hat. Natalie is running her hand over and over the orange streamers attached to the pitcher.

Piper is right behind me. She looks at the cake with the big "10" on it and then back at Natalie through the doorway.

I feel my face get hot. I'm suddenly so angry at my mother, I can barely speak.

"Theresa, Theresa, Theresa," I hear Natalie say.

"Why's she saying that?" I ask my mom.

"Don't ask me. Shame on you, Moose. Go ask your sister," my mother says.

Natalie looks up. Not quite at anybody, but up just the same. "Theresa here," Natalie says. "Theresa."

My mother's face lights up. "Did you hear that, Moose? Did you? Now you move those overgrown feet of yours and invite Theresa over."

I knock on the Mattamans' door. Theresa answers, already in her pajamas. "Of course Natalie wants me, *silly!* We're friends!" she informs me when I tell her what Natalie said.

"Jimmy!" Theresa hollers. She ducks into Jimmy's room and drags him out. Jimmy looks dazed, like he's been living underwater.

"Mommy!" she calls to Mrs. Mattaman. "Jimmy and me are going to the Flanagans'."

Back in our kitchen, we start singing, but before we even get through "birthday," Theresa puts her hand up like a policeman and yells, "Wait! We forgot Annie."

We all look at her.

My mother's cheek twitches a little, like she's not pleased about this. She opens her mouth to object, but too late. Theresa is already out the door.

When Annie arrives, she smiles at us and we all begin singing again. This time we get all the way through.

"Hey, Natalie, did you know your birthday is four months and ten days after Al Capone's," Annie says as my mom cuts the cake.

"January seventeen," Natalie says, "seventeen."

"That's his birthday all right. I made a card for him too," Theresa says. "I cut out little circles to look like bullet holes and everything."

"How did he get that scar, anyway?" I ask.

My father winks at me. "Girl trouble," he says.

My mother starts to open Natalie's presents. I'm not sure why we bother wrapping them. Natalie doesn't understand why presents should be wrapped. If you give her a wrapped gift, she takes it and puts it on her shelf that way.

"Mrs. Flanagan, what are you doing?" Theresa asks.

My mother gets a little red. She flashes her pinched smile. "Natalie doesn't really"—I can almost see her searching for the right word—"care to open her own gifts. . . ."

"Excuse me, Mrs. Flanagan, but that's *my* job." Theresa snatches the half-wrapped present out of my mother's hand and rips the rest of the wrapping off.

"Oh," my mother says. She and my dad exchange a big smile. My mom moves the presents over to where Theresa is sitting.

The first gift is from me. It's a math workbook I got at

school. From Piper she gets a bag of buttons. "Thank you, Piper. These will be for later." My mom winks at Piper, then slips the bag of buttons in her apron pocket.

Theresa gives Nat my father's gift—a book about birds with an enormous index. And from my mother a book bag with NATALIE FLANAGAN, THE ESTHER P. MARINOFF SCHOOL embroidered on the front. My mom doesn't embroider. I don't think she even knows how. "Convicts in the tailor shop," my dad whispers in my ear.

The gifts are all unwrapped now and Natalie is looking at them. She touches each with her fingertips and then sniffs every one. We talk for a while, and when it's time for everyone to leave, my father says, "Moose, walk your friends home, please. Or maybe I should say your harem," he whispers in my ear. "Yours and Jimmy's, that is."

"Give it a rest, Dad," I say.

My dad rumples my hair. His eyes are bright and hopeful.

We all walk together. First we drop off Jimmy and Theresa, then Annie.

"Good night, you two," Annie says to me and Piper. I don't like the way she says this. I pull at my shirt collar, which is pinching my neck.

We walk up the steep road to Piper's house. It's beautiful out. The blue-black night all around, the black, black water, San Francisco like a bright box of lights. This is the most beautiful place I've ever been. Then I look at the cell house, sad and silent. The lights are dim. I don't hear anything except from deep inside the sound of one metal cup clanking the length of the bars and one lone voice calling for help.

"What's that?" I ask, careful not to sound spooked.

"They do that now and then. Usually it's a bunch of them, that way it's hard to tell who's doing it."

"What's the matter?" I ask.

"Who knows," Piper says. When we get to her house, she stops. "How old is she really?" she asks.

I don't say anything.

"Fifteen?" she asks.

"Sixteen," my voice answers. My whole body flames hot and sweaty, then cold.

Piper nods. "That's what we figured," she says.

I walk back down the hill, the word *we* buzzing inside my head like a fly in a small room.

35. THE TRUTH

■ ■

Same day—Monday, May 27, 1935

When I get home, my mom is doing the dishes. Natalie is sitting in the living room, paging through a magazine. For a second there's something so normal about this, until I realize the pages are turning too fast and she's holding the magazine too close to her face. It's the breeze from the spinning pages she's after.

My mom seems more relaxed. The party went well. The day is almost over. Natalie seems fine—as calm as she ever is. I try to walk away. Shut the door of my room. But I can't. Something inside won't let me.

"You can't do this," I tell my mother.

"What?" My mother looks up from the pot she's scouring.

"She isn't ten," I say, my voice hoarse.

My mother winces and turns away. "Yes, she is," she says in a tough voice.

"No, she's not, Mom. She's not and everybody knows it."

My mom continues to stare at the pot. Her face is quivering. Her hands are scrubbing. "She is," she sputters.

"No. Mom. You know she's not."

"Eleven." My mom gulps. She sounds like a very little girl. "I'm going to say she's eleven."

"It's her birthday today. She looks sixteen. She *is* sixteen."

"NO. JUST NO!" my mother roars.

"People know, Mom. They know."

"They don't know!" she cries, tears streaming down her face. "You don't know! She won't have a chance at sixteen. No one will take her. No one cares about an adult that isn't right. It's only kids who have a chance. It's too late if she's sixteen. Don't you see?"

"Yeah, but Mom, you can't pretend! It's worse. People know—"

"No one knows. They don't know and they don't care. Put her in an institution. Do you know how many times I've heard that? Lock her up with all the nuts. She has to be TEN. It's the only chance she has!"

"Don't you think they know at the Esther P. Marinoff? Don't you think Mr. Purdy can tell? Everybody can tell, Mom!"

"No, they can't. She's tall for her age. You're tall too!"

"She's not going to be like everybody else, Mom. This is her only chance and it's no chance at all if you're not honest."

"Don't say it! Don't you dare say anything!" My mom's hands are pressed over her ears.

My father rushes inside. He had been out on the front balcony, chewing his toothpicks. He must have heard us. He looks at my mom, then me. "What the heck is going on here?"

"Natalie is sixteen, Dad. We can't pretend she's not anymore. She isn't ten. She just isn't!"

My dad bites his lip hard. "Let's not do this now, Moose. Not with the interview tomorrow!"

"We have to do it now! Mr. Purdy knows. Everybody does. We can't try to fool them. It won't work. She won't get in."

My father's eyes get big. He shakes his head, but so slowly, he seems to be saying no to what he's thinking, not to me.

It's quiet in the kitchen. My mother is sitting on the step-stool, her face buried in her hands.

My father turns away. I can see by how he covers his head with his hand how ashamed he is of crying.

"Moose," he says, trying to wipe the tears away with his handkerchief. He takes a big noisy breath.

"NO!" My mom cries. "NO!"

Natalie is in the living room, silently rocking.

My dad presses his lips together and wipes at his eyes. He seems to get himself together and breathes a half breath, half sigh. "Moose . . . is right, honey."

"DON'T YOU DARE!" my mother cries.

"Yes," he says again. He puts his arm around my shoulders and walks me out to the living room, where Natalie is sitting, rocking.

"Natalie," he asks softly, his voice breaking. "How old are you?"

"I am sixteen at two thirty-one today," Natalie says, her eyes focused on the table lamp.

My father presses his lips so hard together, they turn white. The tears are falling again, so fast, it looks as if he can't see. He puts his arm around me and pulls me to Natalie. He puts his other arm around her. "I am"—he wipes at his eyes with his shoulder so he doesn't have to let go of us—"so very proud of my children. So very proud." A sob escapes his chest. "What wonderful people you've grown to be."

36. WAITING

The next morning I feel my mother watching me as I rinse my cereal bowl, search for my history homework, put on my socks. She has her makeup on, but her eyes look puffy, her face swollen.

"What?" I ask her.

She says nothing, busies herself getting Natalie ready to go.

When I get home from school, Theresa, Natalie and my mother are sitting in the living room. My mother is radiant. Natalie was wonderful. She spoke clearly in the new Natalie way. She tried her best to look at Mr. Purdy when she spoke. She even told a joke. A joke!

"Why did the chicken cross the road?" my mom said Natalie asked Mr. Purdy.

"Well, I don't know, Natalie," Mr. Purdy had said.

"Because one of his buttons rolled to the other side," Natalie said.

Okay, it wasn't funny. But still.

Even as happy as my mother seems about this, she is still watching me in a way that makes me uncomfortable.

"Come on, Moose," she says after I polish off a stack of cold pancakes from last night's supper. "I want to talk. Just the two of us."

Theresa chatters on about tomato juice. Natalie seems to be listening. I even see her look up at Theresa once or twice. Theresa has a real instinct for what Natalie will find fascinating.

"Who's going to watch Natalie?" I ask. Though really what I'm wondering is what my mom wants to talk about. I don't have talks with my mom. Only with my dad.

"Me, of course," Theresa says.

My mom nods. She smiles at Theresa, but not at me. It's almost as if she doesn't want to look at me.

We walk down the stairs to the dock. She fiddles with the button on her sweater.

"I'm sorry about last night," she says.

What do I say to this? Nothing. I say nothing. I'm too angry to make this easy for her.

She looks across the water to Berkeley. "I didn't like it. I didn't like what you said." She shakes her head.

She dragged me all the way out here to say that? This has to be the biggest understatement in the world.

"You didn't care that it made me mad," my mom says in a quiet tone of voice. "You didn't care that it upset your father. You didn't care that it was the night before Natalie's interview. You didn't care about anything. I have never been so furious with anyone in all my born days." My mom's voice is strangely calm. She isn't angry, but I am. I am seething inside. I open my mouth to tell her how wrong she is, how unfair she's being.

"Wait." She holds her finger to her lips. "Let me finish."

"But I see how much you care about Natalie. That's the part that didn't make sense. All night I tossed and turned. I kept asking why. Moose, of all people. Why did he say that? Why? And you know what? I could only come up with one answer.

"You did it because you believed in your heart it was the right thing to do. You were doing what you thought would help your sister." She stops. Tears spill down her face.

"I can't imagine how I could ask for anything more from you. I can't imagine how I could."

She's crying now, but watching me. Looking at me. I take a swallow of air, like suddenly I have to remind myself to breathe. My mother never does this. She never tries to imagine how I feel. I take another swallow of air and pretend interest in a big barge moving slowly past Angel Island. I don't want to cry.

"Did you tell Mr. Purdy?" I ask. My words come out deep and rich. I hardly recognize my voice.

"No." My mother looks directly at me now. "He didn't ask. And I didn't say. But it's a conversation we need to have. I know that now, Moose." Her voice squeaks. "I do."

That night, my mother makes a wonderful dinner. Roast beef and Yorkshire pudding, green beans with almonds, orange salad, corn bread and cream of asparagus soup. She is just cutting into the lemon meringue pie when we hear the knock.

"Mrs. Caconi!" my dad whispers.

Natalie stops eating. My mom takes a deep breath. She hands me the pie server. My father takes her hand. Together they follow Mrs. Caconi.

Our apartment is suddenly so silent, so empty. Natalie's head moves down close to her plate the way she always used to eat. I only realize now it's been months since I've seen her eat this way. She shovels her pie in one bite after another with no time to chew. I keep eating, but now the pie tastes dull and cold like baby food. I cut myself another piece, but I can hardly chew.

My neck stiffens. It turns to stone. My stomach feels as if I've swallowed a quart of vinegar.

Where are they?

My father's footsteps on the landing are slow and heavy. When he opens the door, his face is sagging and deeply wrinkled. "The decision is the same. *Not ready*," he informs the floor. My dad's shaking hand finds his toothpicks. He pops two in his mouth, goes in his room and closes the door.

37. CARRIE KELLY

■ ■

Same day—Tuesday, May 28, and Wednesday, May 29, 1935

I'm in bed, listening to the sound of my mother crying and the deep even rumble of my father's voice trying to comfort her.

The Esther P. Marinoff is a crummy place. A cruel joke. I never did like that Mr. Purdy.

I try to go to sleep. But I keep thinking about Natalie at home in Santa Monica—living her life in the back room of our house and on the steps of Gram's. I rode bikes with Pete, played ball, did my homework. She did not. I will graduate from high school, go to college, get married, have kids. She will not.

My mom's done a million things to help Natalie. The aluminum treatments, the voodoo dolls, UCLA, the psychiatrists, the Bible readings, Mrs. Kelly. What good were they?

Nothing has helped. But suddenly I see this isn't true. One thing has helped. Carrie Kelly. Natalie has been more a part of things here on this island than she ever has before. She's had a life here, for the first time. Maybe just a little bit of a life. But a life just the same.

When I wake up the next morning, I find Mrs. Kelly's number in my mom's phone book. I borrow a nickel from my dad and head down to the phone outside of Mrs. Caconi's. I put the nickel in the coffee can Mrs. Caconi keeps by the phone and tell the operator the number.

"Mrs. Kelly," I say when the operator signs off, "this is Moose Flanagan, Natalie's brother. I'm calling to thank you. You've really helped my sister."

"Why, dear. I appreciate you saying that."

"And I wanted to ask you. Do you believe the Esther P. Marinoff will help Natalie?"

She sighs. "Yes, I do. I worked there for five years. I saw kids improve in ways I never saw anyplace else I've ever been. Natalie wasn't ready in January, but I think she is now. I'd like her to start in June and I'd like to keep working with her for the first year at least. But unfortunately Mr. Purdy doesn't agree with me."

"Is there anything we can do to change his mind?"

She sighs. "I wish I knew. As I explained to your mother last night, I expected her to be accepted."

"Did her, you know, age . . ." I squeeze the words around the lump in my throat.

"Hard to say. I can certainly understand what your mother was up to with that. There's a real bias against older children. And I can't swear I wouldn't have tried the same thing if I were in her shoes. Sometimes with these kids it's difficult to tell exactly how old they are, but in the case of your sister I'm afraid it's pretty clear she's at least fourteen."

"Yeah," I say in a small voice.

"I will keep working on this, Moose. I promise you I will. But I don't want to give you folks false hope."

"Yes, ma'am," I say.

"And, Moose? There's something I wanted to tell you too, dear. When Natalie and I are working together and I see I'm starting to lose her, I always say, 'What do you think Moose is doing right now?' And lately, she's been able to stay with me.

She talks about you at school or playing catch or talking with Theresa and she's able to keep herself with me that way. I thought you might like to know how important you are to her."

"Yes, ma'am." I wipe the tears off my face.

"I'm sorry I can't do more. You have no idea how sorry I am."

When I hang up the phone, I know I have to do something. Have to. I have no idea what. I wonder if this is how my mother feels. How she has always felt.

Now I understand. When you love someone, you have to try things even if they don't make sense to anyone else.

After breakfast I march up the hill to the warden's house. I don't know why I'm going there, except he's the most powerful person I know. If anyone can change this, he can.

But the closer I get to the warden's house, the slower my feet go. The warden will be at work in the cell house. If I want to talk to him, I'll have to knock on *that* door. I stare at the big steel cell house door, unable to move forward or back. My heart beats in my ear and my hands are ice cold.

I stay stuck until a voice calls my name. "Hey, Moose! What are you doing up here? Aren't you supposed to be in school?"

I spin around to see Mr. Trixle. He has a cigarette in his mouth and a clipboard in his hand.

"Sorry, Moose. Didn't mean to scare you. What's up?"

My mind is whirling. What am I doing? *What am I doing?*

"Moose?" Officer Trixle asks.

"Uh. Yeah. Uh. I need to talk to Warden Williams," I say.

"Can't it wait till tonight, son?" Officer Trixle takes a drag from his cigarette.

"Yes, I mean, no," I mutter.

"Yes, you mean no. Which is it?" He smiles kindly.

"No," I say.

Officer Trixle grunts. He drops his cigarette on the cement and stamps it out with his foot. Then he buzzes the entry bell. The big steel hinges squeak shrill and sharp as the door opens.

"Wait here," Officer Trixle says, and the door slams a solid steel closed behind him.

I wait a long time, wondering if they've forgotten about me. I'm considering giving up when the cell house door squeaks open again and Officer Trixle and the warden appear. The warden is as neat as ever, like he just came out of the barbershop. He smells of soap and cut grass.

"Good morning," he says.

"Good morning, sir," I say.

He looks around as if he doesn't know where to sit. He seems to decide on the bench, gives his trousers a tug and sits down. Officer Trixle walks back to the cell house door and stands stiff and straight, not smoking now.

"So . . ." He folds his hands in his lap. "What's this all about, Moose?"

"W-W-Well, I, uh," I stammer, my forehead suddenly sweaty. "I know you know important people . . . in San Francisco. I was just wondering if you might call some of your, you know, friends and maybe they might ask the Esther P. Marinoff to reconsider. Natalie is doing much better. She should have gotten in."

"Influence, is that what you're after, son?"

"Yes, sir," I say.

"I'll give it some thought, but offhand I can't come up with anyone who might be helpful with this." He sighs and shakes his head. He seems truly sorry.

We sit silent for a moment.

The warden looks at his watch. "Now, it's time you were in school! Bet you can make the eight-thirty if you run like the dickens." He pats my arm and gets up.

"Thanks, sir," I say. "But you know, I had an idea."

He makes a pained noise in his throat.

"I was thinking." My voice cracks. The idea is crazy, but I can't stop myself. "How about Al?"

"Excuse me?" the warden asks.

I clear my throat and try to say it louder, but it still comes out in a croak: "Al Capone."

The warden squints his eyes, just like Piper does. He makes an annoyed sound and shakes his head. "Oh, please don't tell me this is another stunt."

"No, sir. I'm serious. He's the only one who can do this."

"Moose, that's nonsense and I think you know it."

"I think he could."

He sighs a long and labored sigh. "First off, that's doubtful. But even if he could, do you really think I'd allow it? I've built this place on fairness. On treating all of the convicts the same. If I were to ask Al Capone to do me a favor, what kind of precedent would that be setting? He was sent here because he got preferential treatment in Atlanta. Ran his empire from prison while the government footed the bill. Brought his own furniture, Oriental rugs, silk underwear . . . treated him like royalty behind bars. Do you think I want to pave the way for something like that here? It would make a mockery of everything I stand for."

I look directly into his blue eyes. "Remember you said we

should think hard about going against the rules? Remember you said that. Well, I have thought hard."

The warden meets my gaze. "I see that," he says. "But in this case you're asking *me* to bend the rules. And I'm not about to. You may think it's the right thing to do, but I do not."

"You don't have to give him anything. Just ask him. What's the harm of asking, sir?"

The warden takes a deep breath. "Look, Moose, you want to help your sister and that's admirable. But I can't help you with this. Your parents will work something out. Now, run along."

Run along? *Run along?* He can't tell me to act like an adult one moment and treat me like a kid the next. This makes me so furious, my mouth shoots off before I can stop it. "You didn't mean it, did you, sir? It was just a speech. You don't really want us to think, you want us to obey."

I can see the anger flash through the warden's eyes. He takes his foot off the bench and stands straight. "I know you and your family have been through a lot, so I'm going to ignore that comment. But if you speak to me like that again, I will have you and your family off the island in the blink of an eye! Do you understand me?"

"Yes, sir," I say. My whole body trembling.

He continues to stare, then seems to decide I've gotten his point. He sighs and crosses his arms. "Look, son, it isn't that easy. The world isn't going to kiss your boots because you learned to think. You have your answer. It's no. Now, if you'll excuse me, I have things to do."

38. WHAT HAPPENED?

....

The weekend of June 1 and 2, 1935

My mother calls in sick to her piano students and stays in her room. Now when the door opens, a stuffy stale smell comes out and I see her in her bathrobe, her hair tangled like seaweed.

My father is a terrible cook. I look down at my supper plate, fried beets swimming in a pool of bright pink juice, half-cooked hash browns turned pink where they border the beets and cold oatmeal.

My father seems to notice my reaction to his cooking. "If she's still in bed tomorrow, I'll bring home convict cooking. I promise," he says.

"Thanks, Dad," I say.

Natalie is quiet. She has counted the shredded beets on her plate and organized them so they are lying in a line like twenty men in sleeping bags. She seems to be trying to decide what to do with the oatmeal when all of a sudden she blurts out, "Why did the chicken cross the road?"

"I dunno," I say.

"His buttons rolled to the other side," Nat says, picking at her napkin. She looks at me and runs her tongue over her upper lip. Then she wraps her arms around herself, as if she needs them to hold her chest together, and begins to rock. "What happened? What happened?" Natalie asks.

"Nothing happened, Natalie. Mommy isn't feeling well. And we're just not sure the Esther P. Marinoff is the right school for you," my father says.

"Mommy is angry," Natalie says.

My father and I look at each other. His lip quivers and his voice gets gritty. "No, she's not mad at you, honey! You did everything right, Natalie."

"Not mad at you, honey," Natalie says, digging her chin into her collarbone. "Not . . . mad . . . at . . . you . . . honey," she repeats, adding extra pauses between the words.

"Oh, God," my father says. "Natalie, sweetheart, you were great! No one is mad at you!"

But Natalie doesn't look at him. She looks at the butter. Not past it, not through it, but at it, as if it is the most interesting thing in the world.

"You won't believe what I did," I tell Annie and Theresa the next day. "I asked the warden if he'd get Al Capone to help us get Natalie into school."

"You didn't," Annie says.

"I did."

"He said no," Theresa says.

I nod.

"Well, that's a big surprise," Annie says. "You didn't really think he'd say yes, did you?"

I shrug.

"What's Capone going to do, anyway? It's not like he gets out on the weekends to run around town, breaking people's legs," Annie says.

"He could help if he wanted. This is small potatoes for him," I say. "He can do anything."

Annie shakes her head. "The guy's in prison. He can't do *anything*. You've been spending too much time with Piper."

She's right. I know she is. The man's locked up. But this one sentence keeps floating around in my head. *He could if he wanted to. He could if he wanted to.*

It's when I see Piper that I realize what I'm going to do.

"I'm going to write a letter to Al Capone," I tell her.

She rolls her eyes. "They don't let just anyone write to Capone, you know. You have to be a relative and then it's censored."

"Yeah, but it's your mom who censors his mail, right? Couldn't I just drop a letter in the stack of already-censored mail?"

"I've tried that," Piper says, running her fingers through her long hair.

"You did? What happened?"

"Nothin'. Never answered back. I told him to check out *Jane Eyre* from the convict library and put his answer in it."

"*Jane Eyre?* Maybe that was the problem. Can you imagine Al Capone reading *Jane Eyre?*" I ask.

"That's the point, Einstein. A book like that would never be checked out. What con would read *Jane Eyre?* And besides, then my dad wouldn't give me grief for wanting to read it because I had to get him to check it out from the con library for me. I figured Capone could write back in the book—you know, underlining very faintly in pencil the way the cons do."

"No, I don't know."

"Let's say you want to say, 'I need your help.' You go carefully through the book and look for an *I* and underline it. And then an *n* and underline it and an *e* and so on until you've spelled your whole message."

"Did he get it?"

Piper shrugs. "Who knows. I never got an answer back."

"What was the message?"

"I asked him if he'd autograph a baseball and hit it over the wall. I told him I'd auction it off. Said we'd split fifty-fifty."

"Don't you think he has enough money?" I ask.

"No one ever has enough money," Piper says.

"But you didn't get in trouble for this, right, so what's the harm?" I ask.

"Easy for you to say. The only thing your parents did was take away your baseball glove. Not exactly a hardship."

"You're one to talk. You didn't get punished at all."

"Yes, I did. You think I wanted two months with my grandma? She's always crabby and everything she eats is boiled. Boiled cabbage. Boiled turnips. She even boils hamburger."

"I thought you said it was fun."

She rolls her eyes again. "Ever heard of saving face?"

"That's what Annie thought," I say.

"Yeah, well, you should listen to her. She's right most of the time," Piper says.

"Even if you did get in trouble, it doesn't seem to have made any difference to you."

"Oh, yeah? Have I gotten in trouble since then?" Piper asks.

"No," I admit. "Still, wouldn't you like to be Big Al's pen pal? This could be the start."

She snorts like she doesn't care. But her eyes are so bright, I know this isn't true. "What's he going to do to get Natalie in?" she asks.

"Beats me," I say, "but if the guy can fix a whole election, he'll figure out something."

In Piper's room the next day, she brings out the special duplicate carbon letter paper her mom uses. "Can you type?" she asks.

"Nope."

"Me neither. Just, you know, hunt and peck. You don't need to worry if you make mistakes. My mom makes them too. And every once in a while type three dots. That's what she does when she leaves something out. Then, if she happens to glance at your page, she'll think it's a letter she's already finished."

I roll the brown page into her typewriter, click the carriage over and begin hunting down letters with one finger.

```
Dear Mr. Capone,
    I live on Alcatraz. I am Officer
Flanagan's son. My sister Natalie
Flanagan is a little unusual . . .
(Ask Onion 105 about her. He'll tell
you how nice she is.) She needs to be
in a school to help her, but they won't
let her in. It's the Esther P. Marinoff
School in San Francisco . . . Could you
help? The guy who runs it is named Mr.
```

```
Purdy. I would be so grateful if you
could help me with this. Thank you,
sir.


              Sincerely,
              Moose Flanagan


PS I like your mother very much.
```

" 'I like your mother very much'?" Piper says when she reads it.

"You got to say something about the guy's mother."

"Why?" she asks.

"Because then he remembers he has one. And he knows we know her too. Makes him act better. It's The Mom Rule—all guys use it."

"This is Al Capone we're talking about. I don't think he'll fall for a cheap trick like that."

"I'm not taking it out," I say.

"Suit yourself." She takes the letter and presses it in thirds with her thumbnail, making two perfect crisp folds. She disappears with the letter. In less than a minute she's back.

"Piece of cake," she says.

I get up to leave. "Hey, Moose? If this doesn't work, you going back?"

"Back where?"

"Santa Monica, stupid. Not that I care or anything, because I *don't*," she says.

"Well, if you don't care, why are you asking?"

"I'm not asking," Piper says.

"Oh, now you're not asking. Okay, then I'm not answering."

Piper bites at her bottom lip. "Well, are you?"

"I dunno, Piper."

I walk down the stairs. When I get outside, I see Piper watching me through the window of her dad's library. When she sees I see her, she closes the curtain quick and disappears.

39. THE WARDEN

■ ■

Tuesday, June 11, 1935

This last week, things have been better at my house. Natalie is back at Mrs. Kelly's. My mother is teaching piano lessons again and she and my father are beginning to discuss what they will do next. And every day I wonder if we'll be going back to Santa Monica. It seems so long ago that we lived there now, I'm not even sure I want to anymore. And I know moving back will be bad for Natalie.

When I say good-bye to Scout and them on the last day of school, I get a stomachache. I don't know if it's good-bye for the summer or good-bye for the rest of my life. I feel so lousy, I don't say three words to anyone on the boat ride home. I hardly notice anything until I get off the boat.

And then all of a sudden there are my parents, Natalie, Theresa and Warden Williams.

My parents never wait for me like this and it's really strange to see the warden here. He's hardly ever down at the dock. The boat waits for the warden. The warden doesn't wait for the boat. Actually the boat isn't supposed to wait for him either, but it always does.

"What's your dad doing here?" I ask Piper.

"Beats me," Piper says like this is no big deal, but she's chewing her gum at twice the usual speed.

"Guess what!" My mother jumps up the second we're close enough to hear.

"No, wait." Theresa elbows in front of her. "Let Natalie tell."

Natalie frowns down at her feet.

"Go on, Nat, tell him," Theresa says.

"Eleven gulls," Natalie says.

"No, Nat." Theresa shakes her head.

"*Eleven* gulls!" Nat says, louder this time.

"No, I mean . . . yeah, you're right. Eleven gulls," Theresa says. "But what else?"

Natalie's shoulders are hunched up like she is stuck in a shrug. She says nothing.

"She got into the Esther P. Marinoff," Theresa announces with a big grin.

"Natalie!" I wrap my arms around her in a spontaneous bear hug.

"I don't like that! I don't like that," Nat says, and I let go.

"Sorry, Nat," I say.

"Sorry," she says, moving her shoulders now like she's trying really hard to get them to fit. "Sorry, sorry, sorry," she mutters.

"Mr. Purdy called," my dad explains. "He's decided to open another branch of the Esther P. Marinoff for older children and he wants Natalie to be the first student."

"You're sure? I mean, this is for sure?" I ask.

My dad nods. "Apparently he's been planning this for some time—been waiting for the right moment to launch it."

"How come he didn't tell us that before?" I say.

My father looks sideways at my mother. My mother shakes her head. "We don't know," she says.

The warden clears his throat. I can feel the heat of his eyes on me. I glance at him and then away. A patch of sweat breaks out on my forehead.

"See, Moose?" the warden says. "Didn't I tell you your parents would work it out?" He winks at me and smiles out of one side of his mouth. Then he turns his attention to Piper. "Sweetheart, just wanted to tell you how proud I am of your grades. Straight A's *again*." He waves her report card in the air, like he wants us all to see.

"Thank you, Daddy," Piper says as the warden puts his arm around her.

I watch them walk up the hill. When they are out of earshot, I ask my dad, "Just all of a sudden like that?"

My dad nods. He chews at his bottom lip. "You know anything about this, Moose?" he asks.

"No," I answer almost before he gets the question out.

He nods like he believes me, then pops a toothpick in his mouth. "Life is amazing, isn't it? You can't ever tell what will happen. Nobody knows until they go ahead and play the game."

"You can say that again," I say.

40. AL CAPONE DOES MY SHIRTS

▪ ▪

Wednesday, June 12, 1935

The next morning I get up and pull a clean shirt off the hanger. As I shoot my arm through the sleeve, I hear something crackle. I dig my fingers in the pocket and pull out a torn scrap of brown paper. It's folded in half and in half again. Inside is one word scribbled hastily in pencil and underlined twice.

Done, it says.

AUTHOR'S NOTE

....

Alcatraz Island . . . when truth is stranger than fiction.

Al Capone Does My Shirts is a work of fiction, but many of the details about life on Alcatraz are true.

During the twenty-nine years when Alcatraz was a working penitentiary (1934–1963)—or, as one convict described it, "a maximum-security, long-term burying ground for convicts of particularly vile renown"[1]—the families of most of the guards and prison administrators lived on the island. Between fifty and sixty families resided on Alcatraz at any given time. Nine babies were born to mothers who lived on the island and some children lived their entire childhood on Alcatraz.

There was a whole village on the island: a post office with a pelican insignia postmark, a tiny grocery store, a play area called the parade grounds and an Officers' Club complete with a bowling alley. Many of the kids lived in 64 building, an army-issue apartment building that still stands today. No children were ever hurt or taken hostage during the Alcatraz penitentiary years. One guard felt that there was an unwritten "code of rule among the inmates that family men were safe."[2] This may have been true for some convicts, but certainly not all. During the Battle of Alcatraz in May of 1946, two guards were killed and fourteen injured. Almost all were family men. At least one autobiography of an Alcatraz inmate contains detailed escape plans, which included taking the warden's wife as a hostage.[3]

Today it seems surprising that so many children lived on Alcatraz, but at the time Alcatraz was thought to be a better place for kids than the city. "Our parents frequently said they felt safer living on Alcatraz than in San Francisco. There was no traffic, no burglaries; few of us, in fact, worried about security. It was a low-crime neighborhood, after all. Fences and locked gates were everywhere, yet some residents didn't lock their doors."[4] "All of our bad guys are locked up" is a refrain sounded again and again in the handwritten accounts of island life found in the Alcatraz Island Ranger Library.

Also, it was much cheaper to live on Alcatraz. 1935 was a depression year and San Francisco rents, even then, were costly. Prison guards were not highly paid, and as one former Alcatraz guard stated, he "Never even considered living off the island as it was too expensive to live in San Francisco."[5]

But perhaps the most important reason families lived on the island in the early years was because Warden James A. Johnston wanted it this way. Ready access to his staff of guards in the event of a prison break was an important aspect of his overall security plan. High-ranking officers were expected— perhaps even required[6]—to live on Alcatraz. "When we had a disturbance, if we were at a party, we didn't put on our coats or anything, we just went right up the hill. They used to call down at 64 building and the phone was right outside my apartment and we answered the phone and they'd say: 'We have trouble in the cell house,' and that's all they had to say. Everybody available went . . ."[7]

The warden lived in a beautiful mansion located right next

door to the cell house. Warden Johnston (dubbed "Old Salt-water" by the cons) opened Alcatraz and ran it for fourteen years. Warden Johnston's youngest daughter, Barbara, also lived on the island—though she bears no resemblance whatsoever to Piper.

During 1935 all of the Alcatraz kids took the boat to San Francisco, where they attended school. The only exception was made for kindergarten-age children, who attended a kinder-garten held on Alcatraz, taught by one of the moms who lived on the island.[8]

As you might imagine, saying you lived on Alcatraz did, in fact, garner quite a lot of attention at school. Some kids thought it was weird. Others were "dazzled by the prison stories."[9] Most kids who lived on Alcatraz seemed to take the prison for granted. Jolene Babyak, who was a kid on the island during the '50s, said it was like living next to the police station. She said she wasn't scared "because there were so many guards around."[10]

Al Capone (AZ 85) was an inmate on Alcatraz for four and a half years, from 1934 to 1939. Warden Johnston described the intense interest in Capone this way: "The newspaper reporters telephoned me almost every day—'How is Capone? Is he still there? Is he going to be transferred? Where is he working?' " Very little information came out of Alcatraz and erroneous re-porting was rampant. "At times," Warden Johnston said, "I be-came fed up with the gossip about him that had no foundation in fact. . . . A story was featured that though Al Capone was in Alcatraz, he was sending orders to a London haberdasher for silk underwear . . . I assured the Director of the Bureau of Prisons that there was no truth in such a report . . . that I had seen Capone wearing the regulation underwear and I had noticed it particularly because he had the waist of his drawers fastened with a safety pin."[11]

The residents of the island were as interested in Capone as the rest of the world. One boy described watching Capone's first footsteps on Alcatraz: "Our apartment overlooked the island's docks, and my mother's old Kodak box camera took a photo of the first convicts' arrival. We lived along the building's upper gallery, but we went down a level to be closer to the action that we had waited months to see. Our binoculars located Al Capone, his face was familiar in those days. No others stood out."[12] Another woman said: "The first prisoners arrived, among them Al Capone." She laughed. "And women and children were requested to stay indoors until the prisoners were locked in their cells. . . . Well, we kind'a snuck a look before the boat docked."[13]

Capone's first job on Alcatraz was working the mangle in the laundry facility[14]—thought to be an undesirable post often offered as a first job because it was boring, backbreaking work. The facility handled the laundry for everyone who lived on the island and for some of the local army bases, like the one on Angel Island.

The laundry scheme is fiction. No record of kids selling the opportunity to have a shirt laundered by Capone has ever been found. However, there is documentation of at least one army officer—a private stationed on Angel Island—writing home that "his laundryman was Al Capone."[15]

In fact, after completing *Al Capone Does My Shirts,* I discovered that World War II GIs sometimes used the phrase "Al Capone does my shorts"[16] to indicate they were stationed in San Francisco. Capone was no longer on Alcatraz then, but the "Capone mythology"[17] was as powerful as ever.

In 1935, the convicts played handball and softball in the walled-off recreation yard on the island, and Capone was thought to have played first base.[18] Capone liked baseball. As a kid, he "pitched sandlot baseball well enough to cherish dreams of turning pro."[19] The convicts were quite serious about their games and kept careful records of their leagues. "They played as avidly as any big league team out to win the pennant."[20] But the rules differed from those of a regular game in one important way. On Alcatraz "If you knocked the ball over the wall, you're out. (It was not a home run and you couldn't get out and get it, either.) We usually had an inmate that worked outside the wall—the gardener. He would throw them back."[21]

The kids who lived on the island did, in fact, collect convict handballs and baseballs. "Once when I was eight, a prisoner found a hard rubber ball in the weeds and beckoned to me. I shyly approached, as the guard stood there, and the man pushed the ball through the fence to me. It was a proud moment; I had in my hand *the* most valuable item on Alcatraz—the coveted black handball that had rolled down the hill from over the prison yard wall."[22]

Many of the other details of Capone's time on Alcatraz are also true. There was, for example, a snitch box, which visitors and residents alike were required to walk through when entering the island. And when Capone's mother, Teresina Capone, came to visit him on the island, her corset did indeed set the snitch box off. "Mrs. Capone, who barely spoke English, was visibly embarrassed at having to strip down to her corset, revealing the metal stays that had tripped the metal detector."[23]

Capone was horribly ruthless, authorizing and sometimes performing the slaying of hundreds of people, but he could also be surprisingly generous. "When the crash came in 1929, he (Al Capone) was first to open soup kitchens."[24] Some people considered him a Robin Hood kind of character[25]—or, as one fellow Alcatraz convict described him, "Outside of losing his head so easily and bragging about what he has done, Capone has a heart as big as a house."[26]

The accounts of children who grew up on Alcatraz differ according to the time they lived on the island and their own individual experiences. A doctor who worked on the island in 1937 said, "During their play, the children often came into close contact with the prisoners working on the outdoor details."[27] On the other hand, one former Alcatraz island resident whom I heard speak clearly stated she had no interaction with convicts whatsoever during her stay on the island. And a third said she formed a friendship with one convict based on the exchange of flowers. She called this inmate her "boyfriend."[28]

The convicts' mail was routinely censored and wives of the guards were occasionally asked to help out with this task. As one convict described it: "It took a letter from ten days to two weeks to get to you after it reached the institution. You see, all the incoming letters are censored and then given to different guards to type in duplicate when they have time. Nothing was personal. Every officer could take your letters and read them and then discuss your personal affairs with each other. The prisoners' personal mail was taken home by different officers to let their wives read."[29]

Incredible though it seems, residents of the island sang Christmas carols outside of the cell house with the express purpose of entertaining the convicts. As one woman who lived on the island during the early '40s told me, caroling was a very big thing. And only the children who were the best singers were given the privilege of caroling to the cons.[30]

And it is certainly true that convicts were sometimes seen in the residential areas of the island. They were on the dock handling the laundry. They acted as garbagemen, gardeners, and sometimes movers and house painters for the guards who lived on the island. And while it is true that convicts were always supposed to be escorted by guards, it is certainly conceivable that in some cases that rule would have been bent or broken.

Meeting Capone was a big thrill to kids who lived on the island. One ten-year-old boy described the day he met Capone.

> On rare occasions dependents entered the prison proper. I became a more familiar figure because Doctor Hess, or medical assistant Charles Ping, gave me adrenaline shots for asthma. Of course, my father escorted me to and from the prison hospital/dispensary. On the notable occasion, Capone was being treated, and my father's sense of history came through.
>
> He said, "Al, this is my boy, Roy.
>
> "Rollo," Dad's nickname for me, "this is Al Capone."
>
> Capone shook my hand and I said something and, I suppose, twitched around the way ten-year-olds do.
>
> Capone said, "Good-looking boy, Boss."
>
> That was a big moment for a boy, and I can still recall the warmth of Capone's hand around mine.[31]

Though every attempt was made to make *Al Capone Does My Shirts* historically accurate, some details were changed to suit the story. For example, the weather—while true to the San

Francisco Bay area in general—does not reflect the exact weather of 1935. Also, the island was run in "rigid military style,"[32] with orders working their way down the chain of command. Talking to a kid about the rules of the island would probably be something the warden would have delegated. And though the concept of separate schools for children with problems was certainly in existence,[33] everything else about the Esther P. Marinoff School is completely fictional.

About Natalie

The character Natalie Flanagan would probably be diagnosed with autism. Autism is a disease that affects the way your brain and sensory system work. It usually becomes evident in the first three years of a child's life.[34] While there is a whole range of behaviors of people with autism, typically a child with autism has an extremely difficult time making eye contact, playing with other kids and sometimes even speaking. Children with autism are often prone to tantrums, repetitive behaviors and intense physical sensitivities and desensitivities, "some sensations being heightened and even intolerable, others (which may include pain perception) being diminished or apparently absent."[35]

Temple Grandin, perhaps the most famous person with autism in the world today, says autism is "A near normal brain trapped inside a sensory system that does not work."[36] Noted autism experts Theodore and Judith Mitrani describe autism as "Extreme aloneness from the beginnings of life."

Autism wasn't identified until 1943, a full eight years after this book takes place. Children with what we now call autism received many different diagnoses during the 1930s and were sometimes institutionalized. Up until quite recently there was little hope for children with autism. As Oliver Sacks put it, "We almost always speak of autistic children, never of autistic adults, as if such children never grew up, or were somehow mysteriously spirited off the planet."[37] But in the last few years a lot of progress has been made in the treatment of autism. The most encouraging statistics show that intense early intervention with applied behavioral analysis can help as many as half the children diagnosed with autism to achieve normal functioning.[38]

Natalie is a wholly fictional character. She is not meant to symbolize or represent autism in any way. She was inspired by my own sister, Gina Johnson, who had a severe form of autism.

NOTES

1 AL BEST [pseud.], *"Inside Alcatraz: The Prison Memories of Inmate Number 107: The Untold Story of Al Capone on the Rock,"* ed. Richard Reinhardt, *San Francisco Focus,* December 1987, 76.

2 Unpublished Alcatraz notebooks. Accounts of life on Alcatraz written by Alcatraz residents. Rangers, docents and volunteers on Alcatraz have access to this information in order to prepare programs for the public. I worked as a volunteer docent on Alcatraz from October 1998 through November 1999.

3 ALVIN KARPIS, *On the Rock: Twenty-five Years in Alcatraz: The Prison Story of Alvin Karpis As Told to Robert Livesey* (Don Mills, Ont.: Musson Book, 1980), 110.

4 JOLENE BABYAK, *Eyewitness on Alcatraz: True Stories of Families Who Lived on the Rock* (Berkeley, Calif.: Ariel Vamp Press, 1988), 4.

5 Unpublished Alcatraz notebooks.

6 Ibid.

7 BABYAK, *Eyewitness on Alcatraz,* 66.

8 ROY F. CHANDLER and E. F. CHANDLER, *Alcatraz, the Hard Years, 1934–1938* (Orwigsburg, Pa.: Bacon and Freeman, 1989), 86–87.

9 BABYAK, *Eyewitness on Alcatraz,* 3.

10 JOLENE BABYAK, daughter of Arthur Dollison, Associate Warden on Alcatraz, during a conversation with me on January 21, 2002.

11 JAMES A. JOHNSTON, *Alcatraz Island Prison, and the Men Who Live There* (Douglas/Ryan Communication, 1999), 31.

12 CHANDLER and CHANDLER, *Alcatraz, the Hard Years,* 29.

13 BABYAK, *Eyewitness on Alcatraz,* 12.

14 JOHNSTON, *Alcatraz Island Prison, and the Men Who Live There,* 41.

15 Ibid., 41.

16 JOHN A. MARTINI, author of *Fortress Alcatraz: Guardian of the Golden Gate,* in a phone conversation with me on January 23, 2003.

17 Ibid.

18 BEST, "Inside Alcatraz," 130.

19 ROBERT J. SCHOENBERG, *Mr. Capone: The Real—and Complete—Story of Al Capone* (New York: Morrow, 1992), 21.

20 MILTON DANIEL BEACHER, M.D., *Alcatraz Island: Memoirs of a Rock Doc,* ed. Dianne Beacher Perfit (Lebanon, N.J.: Pelican Island Pub., 2001), 67.

21 FRANK HEANEY and GAY MACHADO, *Inside the Walls of Alcatraz* (Palo Alto, Calif.: Bull, 1987), 52.

22 BABYAK, *Eyewitness on Alcatraz,* 18.

23 Ibid., 13.

24 SCHOENBERG, *Mr. Capone,* 179.

25 Ibid.

26 BEST, "Inside Alcatraz," 124.

27 BEACHER, *Alcatraz Island: Memoirs of a Rock Doc,* 128.

28 "Kids on the Rock" presentation given by people who grew up on Alcatraz, Alcatraz Alumni Day, August 12, 2001.

29 BEST, "Inside Alcatraz," 80.

30 "Kids on the Rock" presentation.

31 CHANDLER and CHANDLER, *Alcatraz, the Hard Years,* 31–32.

32 JOLENE BABYAK in a letter to me dated February 13, 2003.

33 In 1936, a year after the book takes place, the city of San Francisco opened a school for children with "special" problems. According to the 1936 Report of the Superintendent of the San Francisco Public Schools, the school—called the Sunshine School—was for children "for whom we cannot do too much in the attempt to help them overcome their handicaps."

34 Autism Society of America Web site, "What is Autism," accessed April 28, 2003 [http://www.autism-society.org].

35 OLIVER SACKS, *An Anthropologist on Mars: Seven Paradoxical Tales* (New York: Knopf, 1995), 245.

36 TEMPLE GRANDIN, *Thinking in Pictures: And Other Reports from My Life with Autism* (New York: Vintage Books, 1996), 53.

37 OLIVER SACKS, foreword to *Thinking in Pictures: And Other Reports from My Life with Autism,* by Temple Grandin, 11–12.

38 Families for Early Autism Treatment–North Texas Web site, "What scientific evidence supports Intensive Behavioral Intervention," accessed April 28, 2003 [http://www.featnt.org/info/brochure.asp]: "Given an average of 40 hours per week of one-on-one treatment for 2 or more years, 47% of the children recovered to the point of being indistinguishable from their normal developing peers."